"I want you, Sun

Bryce cupped her face in his hands as he continued, "I'd marry you right this minute if I could." His eyes blazed into hers, commanding her full attention.

Bryce's desire for her sizzled into Sunny's bloodstream, bringing a vibrancy that reenergized her whole body.

"Then I will...I will marry you, Bryce," she heard herself say, as though the words were drawn from a place she was barely conscious of, yet she knew even as she said them, she wouldn't take them back.

This is Australian author **Emma Darcy's** 75th *Harlequin Presents®* novel. Her intense, passionate, fast-paced writing style has made Emma Darcy hugely popular with readers: she's sold nearly 60 million copies of her books worldwide. Emma is also the author of the international bestseller *The Secrets Within,* published by MIRA® Books.

Look out in October for Emma Darcy's next Harlequin Presents novel:

Claiming His Mistress (#2206)

Pick up a Presents Passion—
where seduction is *guaranteed!*

Coming in October:

Christos's Promise
by Jane Porter
Harlequin Presents #2210

Emma Darcy

THE HOT-BLOODED GROOM

Passion™

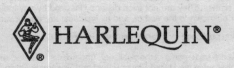

HARLEQUIN®

TORONTO • NEW YORK • LONDON
AMSTERDAM • PARIS • SYDNEY • HAMBURG
STOCKHOLM • ATHENS • TOKYO • MILAN • MADRID
PRAGUE • WARSAW • BUDAPEST • AUCKLAND

ISBN 0-373-12195-4

THE HOT-BLOODED GROOM

First North American Publication 2001.

CHAPTER ONE

'I WANT you married.'

Bryce Templar gritted his teeth. It wasn't the first time his father had made this demand. Undoubtedly it wouldn't be the last, either. But he hadn't come out of his way to visit the old man, still convalescing from his recent heart operation, to have another argument about his bachelor state.

He kept his gaze trained on the view, ignoring the contentious issue. The sun was setting, adding even more brilliant shades of colour to the stunning red rocks of Sedona. His father's winter residence was certainly sited to capture one of the most striking panoramas nature had to offer, here in the Arizona desert. And of course, communing with nature was another thing Will Templar preached—spiritual peace, clean air, clean living…

'Are you hearing me, boy?'

Bryce unclenched his jaw and slid his father a derisive look. 'I'm not a boy, Dad.'

'Still acting like one,' came the aggressive grumble. 'Here you are with your hair going grey and you're not settled with a woman yet.'

'I'm only thirty-four. Hardly over the hill. And you went grey in your thirties. It's genetic.'

It wasn't the only physical aspect of his father he'd inherited. They were both well over six feet tall, big men, though his father had lost quite a bit of weight over the past year and was looking somewhat gaunt in the face. They had the same strong nose, the same determined mouth, closely set ears, and while his father's hair was now white, it was still as thick as his own.

The only feature he'd inherited from his mother was her eyes—heavier lidded than his father's and green instead of grey. Will Templar's eyes had been described in print as steely and incisive, but right now they were smoking at Bryce with irritable impatience.

'I was married to your mother in my twenties.'

'People married earlier in those days, Dad.'

'You're not even looking for a wife.' He shook an admonishing finger. 'You think I don't hear about your bed-hopping with starlets in L.A.? Getting laid indiscriminately doesn't sit well with me, son.'

Bryce barely stifled a sigh as he thought, *Here comes the clean living lecture.* 'I don't bed-hop and I'm not indiscriminate in my choice of playmate,' he bit out. Hoping to avoid a diatribe on morals, he added, 'You know how busy I am. I just don't have the time to put into a relationship what women want out of it.'

It brought his father up from his lounger in a burst of angry energy. 'Don't tell me women don't want marriage. They all want marriage. It's not difficult to get a woman to say *yes* to that. And I'm living proof of it with five wives behind me.'

All of them walking away with a bundle, Bryce thought cynically. Except his mother who died before she'd got around to divorce. The billion dollar empire

of Templar Resources could ▊
dreds of wives. It just so happe▊
the idea of being taken for the po▊
of the rainbow ride.

If a woman wanted him…fine. ▊
wanted her. But the occasional pleasu▊
not warrant a gold ring and a gold passpo▊ ▊efty
divorce settlement. Apart from which, he certainly
didn't need the aggravation of a demanding wife. He
much preferred a walkaway situation.

'You get married, Bryce, or I'll put Damian in control of business, right over your head. Make him CEO
until you do get a wife. That will free up your time,'
his father threatened.

'And give you another heart attack when he messes
up,' Bryce mocked, knowing his half-brother's lim-
ited vision only too well.

'I mean it, boy! Time's slipping by and I'm feeling
my mortality these days. I want to see you married,
and married soon. With a grandchild on the way, too.
Within a year. Just get out there and choose a wife.
You hear me?'

He was going red in the face. Concerned about his
father's blood pressure, Bryce instantly set aside the
argument. 'I hear you, Dad.'

'Good! Then do it! And find a woman like your
mother. She had a brain, as well as being beautiful.'
He sank back onto the cushions of the lounger, taking
quick shallow breaths. The high colour gradually re-
ceded. 'Worst day of my life when your mother died.'

Bryce couldn't remember it. He'd only been three
years old. What he remembered was the succession

...pmothers who had waltzed into and out of his
childhood and adolescence.

'Got to think of the children,' his father muttered.
'Damian's mother was a featherhead. Charming, sexy,
but without a thought worth listening to.' His eyes
closed and his voice dropped to a mumble. 'Damian's
a good boy. Not his fault he hasn't got your brain. At
least he's guidable.'

Watching fatigue lines deepen on his face, making
him look older than his sixty years, Bryce was troubled by the thought there was more to his father's
remark on *feeling his mortality* than he was letting
on. Just how bad was his heart condition?

While they'd had this argument over marriage before, there'd never been a time-frame stipulated.

Within a year.

And the threat about Damian—empty though it
was—added more weight to the demand, carrying a
measure of desperation.

The sun had slipped below the horizon as they'd
talked. The massive red rocks were darkening with
shadows. Nothing stayed the same for long, Bryce
reflected, and if time was running out for his father...well, why not please him by getting married?

It shouldn't be too much of a problem.

He wouldn't let it be.

CHAPTER TWO

SUNNY YORK's heart did not leap with joy when she spotted her fiancé shoving through the crowd of delegates waiting to enter the conference room. His appearance sent a shudder of distaste down her spine and she found herself gritting her teeth as a host of blistering criticisms clamoured to be expressed.

It was the last day of the conference, the last day to try and smooth over the bad impressions he'd made on others, and the most important day for her, which Derek knew perfectly well. And he turned up like this?

She shook her head in disgust, thinking of how early she had risen this morning, determined on presenting a perfect, go-getting image. It had taken an hour to get her unruly mane of rippling curls under reasonable control, carefully blow-drying out any tendency to frizz and ensuring the whole tawny mass of it looked decently groomed. Her make-up was positive without being overdone, and her sharp yellow suit was a statement of vibrant confidence.

There was absolutely nothing sharp about Derek. His suit looked rumpled, as though he'd dropped it on the floor and dragged it on again. His eyes were bloodshot, he'd nicked his chin shaving, and he was obviously in no state to get anything out of the morning session. She actually bristled with rejection as he hooked his arm around hers.

'Made it,' he said, as though it were an achievement she should be grateful for.

Never mind that he'd broken every arrangement for them to spend private time together. Turning up for her sales presentation did not make up for treating her like nothing all week. And turning up like this was the last straw to Sunny.

Her sherry-brown eyes held no welcoming warmth as she tersely replied, 'I expected to see you at breakfast.'

He leaned over confidentially. 'Had it at the roulette table. Free drinks, free food all night. They sure look after you at these casinos and I was running hot.'

Sunny's heart felt very cold. 'I'm amazed you tore yourself away.'

He grimaced as though *she* was acting like a pain to him. 'Don't nag. I'm here, aren't I?'

Four days they'd been in Las Vegas and he'd been gambling every spare minute, even skipping conference sessions when he thought he could get away with it. 'I take it the hot run ended,' she bit out, barely controlling a fiery flash of temper at *his* criticism of *her* attitude.

'Nope. I won a packet,' he slurred smugly. 'But I happened to see the big man come in last night and if he's showing this morning…'

'What big man?' she snapped, losing all patience with him.

'The head of the whole shebang. Bryce Templar

himself. He dropped into the L.A. conference last year to give us a pep talk, remember?'

Sunny remembered. The CEO of Templar Resources was the most gorgeous hunk she'd ever seen, almost a head taller than she was and with a big muscular frame that telegraphed *all man* to her, eminently lust-worthy, but so far beyond her reach, he was strictly dream material.

She hadn't heard a word he'd said at L.A. She'd sat in the audience, imagining how it might be in bed with all that strong maleness being driven by the charismatic energy he was putting out in his address to them.

His father had founded Templar Resources, back in 1984, and it was now the largest networking company in the world, producing and servicing software in most languages. Obviously the son was building on that, not just inheriting his position, which added even more power to his sex appeal. On any male evolution scale he was definitely the top rung.

'Guess he'll do the same today,' Derek babbled on. 'Thought I'd better turn up for it.'

Sunny cast a severely jaundiced look at the man she'd cast in the future role of her husband and father to the family she wanted. Having seen her two younger sisters married and producing adorable babies, she'd become hopelessly clucky, and when Derek had walked into her life, he'd seemed the answer to her dreams.

Those dreams had received an awful lot of tarnishing this week, and right at this moment, the reminder of a man as powerfully impressive as Bryce Templar did nothing to shine them up again.

Derek was the same height as herself—if she wore flat heels—and quite handsome on better days when his blue eyes were clear and his face more alive. His dark blond hair was still damp from a very recent shower so the sun-bleached streaks weren't showing so much this morning. He usually kept his rather lean physique toned up with sessions in the gym but he hadn't been anywhere near the hotel's health club this week.

All in all, he was much less a man in Sunny's eyes than he'd been four days ago. Whether this gambling fever was a temporary madness or not, he'd completely lost her respect, and she'd hand him back his diamond ring right now, except it might cause a scene that she could do without in front of the other delegates whose respect *she* wanted when she gave her presentation in just another hour's time.

Deeply disillusioned and angry with the assumption she would overlook everything, she unhooked her arm from Derek's as they moved into the conference room and gave him a stony warning. 'Don't think you can lean on me if you fall asleep.'

'Oooh, we are uptight, aren't we?' he mocked, looking uglier by the second. 'Nervous about performing in front of the CEO?'

'No. I just don't want to prop you up,' she grated.

'Fine! Then I'll sit at the back and you won't have to worry about it,' he sniped, sheering away from her side in a blatant huff.

Sunny walked on, rigidly ignoring him. No doubt

a back-row seat suited Derek very well. If Bryce Templar didn't show, he could easily slip outside and get on with his gambling. Though if he thought other people besides herself hadn't noticed what was going on, he was a fool.

The managing director of the Sydney branch had already commented on his absence from conference sessions, as well as his failure to attend any of the social functions at night. Derek might be considered a top consultant but playing the corporate game was important, too. He was earning a big black mark here in Las Vegas, not only on a personal level, but a professional one, as well.

Still inwardly fuming over his behaviour, Sunny made her way to the very front row of tables in the auditorium, where she was entitled to sit as one of the presenters this morning. Having settled herself and greeted the other delegates in the team she'd been attached to all week, she did her best to push Derek's disturbing behaviour out of her mind, concentrating on listening to the buzz about Bryce Templar's arrival on the scene.

Had he come to announce some new technologies being developed by the company? Was he here to reward someone for outstanding performance? Speculation was running rife.

It ended abruptly as the man himself made his entrance, accompanied by the conference organisers. A hush fell over the room, attention galvanised on the CEO of Templar Resources. He took the podium without any introduction but whatever he said floated right over Sunny's head.

From a purely physical viewpoint, she couldn't help thinking that Bryce Templar had to have the best gene pool in the whole world, and if she could choose any one man to be the father of the baby she'd love to have, he would top the stud-list.

The woman in yellow kept attracting Bryce's eye. She was the only spot of colour amongst a sea of grey and black business clothing. Since she was seated right at the front, he couldn't miss seeing her, and as women went, she was definitely worth a second look.

Great hair. Lush wide mouth. Big dreamy eyes. A strong impression of warmth, which stayed with him as he left the podium, niggling at the bitterness his lawyer had stirred with the call about yet another change Kristen was demanding in the prenuptial agreement. His fiancée was fast dissipating any warmth he'd felt for her.

As he sat down at the official table with the conference organisers, he reflected on the black irony of having thought he'd picked the ideal wife. Kristen Parrish had enough beauty and brains to meet his father's criteria, plus a very stylish career as an interior decorator, which meant she wouldn't be hanging on having a husband dance attendance all the time. She had a business of her own to run. Which suited Bryce just fine.

The problem was, her sharp brain was proving to be one hell of a calculating machine, and Bryce fiercely resented the way she was manipulating the situation. Just one mention that he wanted a child, preferably within the first year of marriage, and she'd started using it as a bargaining chip to ensure she would always have funds to raise their child should the marriage fail. She was literally bleeding him for all she could get, and if it wasn't for his father, he'd tell her to get lost.

Then she'd probably sue him for breach of promise.

And would he find anyone better?

His gaze flicked to the woman in yellow and caught her looking at him. Her head instantly jerked away, thick dark lashes swept down, and her cheeks bloomed with heat. Quite an amazing blush. She had to be in her late twenties or early thirties, and very committed to a career to be here at this conference. Hardly the shy type. She wouldn't be wearing yellow if she was shy.

Her cheeks were still burning, lending even more vivid colour and warmth to her face. It was a very appealing, feminine face, finely boned, though not quite perfect with the slightly tip-tilted nose. Her hair drew his attention again, copper and corn colours tangled through a tousled riot of waves and curls, the thick mass of it falling from a centre parting and tumbling down over her shoulders. It looked...very touchable, unlike Kristen's ice-blond sculptured bob.

He wondered what the woman in yellow would be like in bed, then put a firm clamp on those thoughts.

He'd made his bed.

Besides, would the woman in yellow prove any different to Kristen when it came to the money angle?

With a cynical shake of his head, Bryce reached

for a glass of iced water. No point in getting heated about anyone he didn't know...or Kristen's greed.

His forthcoming marriage was a done deal. Almost a done deal. He didn't have the time to settle with someone else. The doctors had told him it was a miracle his father was still alive and they were using experimental drugs to treat his condition. Such risky medication held out no guarantees, and Bryce didn't want to delay giving what peace of mind this marriage might bring, at least in the short term.

No point in brooding over the outcome for himself, either. He'd flown to Vegas to hand out awards and get a feel of how the rank and file were dealing with the company products. His mission this morning was to listen and observe. Which he proceeded to do.

First up was a panel who role-played selling the concepts of particular products to customers who have no idea how they would work in business, or that they even existed to be used. Bryce was favourably impressed by their understanding and the concise way they focused on customer needs to adopt and apply more profitable business practices.

Next came a sample presentation to a company board level, delivered by a Business Development Manager from Sydney, Australia. The program noted that Sunny York had the enviable record of always achieving her quota of sales. *Her*...a woman? His interest piqued, Bryce waited curiously to assess why she was so successful.

The conference organiser finished his patter on her, raised his arm in a welcoming gesture, and in a typically hyped-up voice, announced, 'Miss Sunny York.'

Up stood the woman in yellow!

She had a smile on her face that would captivate and dazzle even the hardest-headed financial directors. And she was tall—six feet tall, Bryce estimated—and more than half of that height was taken up by the longest legs he'd ever seen on a woman. He couldn't help watching them as she stepped up to the podium. Her skirt ended above her knees but it wasn't a mini. It simply looked like a mini on those legs, and she wasn't even wearing high-heels, just comfortable court shoes with enough of a heel to look elegant.

His gaze travelled slowly upwards from her feet...what would it be like to have those long, shapely legs wrapped around him...the curvy cradle of her hips underneath him...plenty of cushion in those nicely rounded breasts, too...that mouth, so full-lipped and wide, made for sensual pleasure...and her hair tumbling everywhere.

'Hi!' She spread her smile and twinkling eyes around the audience, drawing everyone to her with a flow of warmth that sparked responding smiles. 'I'm here to help you make money...and save money.'

She had them in her hand from that very first delivery and didn't let them go for one second in the whole forty minutes of her presentation. It didn't feel like a hard-sell. She came over as concerned to serve the customer's very best interests, her voice carrying a very natural charm, allied to a mobility of expression which was almost mesmerising. The line of logic she injected into selling sounded so simple and convincing, she left no doubt this was a winning move, and her own positive energy literally generated positive energy through the whole auditorium.

Bryce found himself totally entranced.

Even her Australian accent was endearing.

Sunny...

He could certainly do with a bit of that sun in his life. A lot of it. All of it. His stomach clenched as his mind skidded to Kristen. He didn't want a cool-headed calculator. Taking her as his wife went against every grain in his entire body...and that very same body was craving what Sunny York might give him.

His eyes feasted on her as she stepped down from the podium. He'd invite her to join him for lunch...test possibilities. Seize the day. Seize the night. A night with Sunny York would at least satisfy the compelling fantasies she'd been stirring, and if she was all she promised to be...

The flash of a diamond on her left hand pulled the hot run of thoughts up with a jolt. Bryce stared at the ring that declared Sunny York was engaged to be married, committed to another man, whom she probably loved. Her whole performance demonstrated she put her heart into everything she did. Heart and soul.

Bryce wasn't used to feeling like a loser. It hit him hard, the sick hollowness following on the wild surge of excitement she had evoked in him. He sat back in his chair and grimly reviewed his options.

He might be able to seduce her away from her fiancé. Inducements marched through his mind...

powerful attractions for most women. But if he did
win her like that...would he still want her?

Give it up, man, he told himself savagely.

Kristen was ready and willing...so long as he paid
the price she demanded. Which he could well afford.

Settle with her and be done with it.

CHAPTER THREE

SUNNY headed for the ground-floor casino, determined on having a showdown with Derek. He hadn't come to the lunch—not even waiting outside the conference room to give her a courtesy comment on her presentation before skipping off—and he hadn't shown for the last session, regardless of the fact that Bryce Templar had been giving out awards. His respect for *the big man* obviously hadn't extended that far.

She didn't like the casino floor. The assault on her ears from countless bell-ringing slot machines was horrific. It was bad enough walking through it. Actually spending hours here was beyond her understanding. Having finally located the roulette tables, she scanned them for Derek and was frustrated at not finding him. Could he have gone to bed—the need for sleep catching up with him?

Frowning, Sunny moved from foot to foot, too worked up to walk away with so much angst playing through her mind. She shot her gaze in every direction, not really expecting to resolve anything, simply at a loss to know what to do next. It came as a shock when she actually spotted Derek, seated at a *blackjack* table, watching the cards being played by the dealer with an intensity that cramped her heart.

He was caught in a thrall that nothing was going to break.

It seemed that nothing else mattered.

Sickened by the realisation of how destructively addictive gambling could be, Sunny hesitated over confronting Derek, yet the relationship they had shared up until this week demanded that he at least recognise how he was treating it. The need to get through to him drove her over to the blackjack table. She waited until he threw down his cards in disgust, apparently having lost his bet, then tapped him on the shoulder.

'Derek...'

He sliced an impatient frown at her.

'...could I speak to you, please?'

'Can't you see I'm playing?'

'It's important.'

Grimacing at the interruption, he heaved himself off his chair and tipped the back of it onto the edge of the table to hold his place. 'What's so damned important?' he demanded, his bleary eyes snapping with frustration.

'It's the last night...'

'I've just lost the roll I won at roulette. My luck's got to turn...'

'Derek, we've got seats for the *Jubilee* show. And dinner beforehand.'

'The action is here. I'm not leaving it.'

'Don't I mean anything to you anymore?' she cried, trying to get through the obsessive glaze to some grain of perspective on what he was doing.

The personal tack clearly irritated him. 'I sat

through your presentation. You slayed 'em as you always do. Is that what you want to hear?' he said ungraciously, then waved a sharp dismissal as he added, 'If you're hot to go and watch some showgirl extravaganza, fine. But as you just pointed out, this is our last night here and I want to win my money back.'

'And what if you don't? What if you lose more?'

He looked shifty.

'Derek, just how much have you lost already?'

Feverish need flashed at her. 'I'll win it back. It's only a matter of time.'

An icy fear struck her. 'Have you been gambling on credit?'

'That's my business. We're not married yet.'

No sharing. No desire to share. Complete shut-out. Hurt and disappointment held her silent for a moment as she realised beyond any doubt that there could be no happy future for them. A bitter urge to show him what he'd done, how low he had fallen, had her wrenching the diamond ring off her finger.

'Here!' She held it out to him. 'You can pawn it. Get some more money to throw down the drain.'

It rocked him. 'Now look here, Sunny...'

'No. Try looking at yourself, Derek. It's over for me.'

'Well, if you feel that way...' His eyes glittered as he took the ring. 'You'll change your mind when I win a bundle.'

He was unreachable on any level. 'I won't change my mind. We're through, Derek,' she said with absolute finality.

His gaze had dropped to the diamond in his hand,

and Sunny had the gut-wrenching impression he was assessing what he could get for it. Her eyes blurred— all the inner torment of hopes and dreams being just swept away suddenly catching her by the throat. For their eight-month-long relationship to come to this...

She swung away, swallowing hard to stop herself from bursting into tears and making a spectacle of herself. Her legs moved automatically, driven by the need to get out of the casino, out of this dreadful playground which trapped people and drained them of any soul she could relate to.

The slot machines jangled around her, a cacophony of sound that seemed to mock her misery. She completely lost her bearings, not knowing what direction led to an exit. A moment's enforced reasoning told her to head for the hotel's reception desk from where the lobby was definitely in view.

It was such a relief to break free of the vast gambling area, tears swam into her eyes again. This time she simply put her head down and followed the walkway to the lobby, hoping not to run into anyone who knew her.

The limousine was waiting. His plane was waiting to fly him back to L.A. Kristen was waiting for him to return to her, no doubt ready to sweeten her prenuptial demands with how well she would accommodate his needs. Bryce Templar told himself that what he'd just witnessed didn't change anything, but still he lingered in the lobby, watching Sunny York.

She'd taken off the diamond ring.

The man she'd handed it to wasn't following her.

Her haphazard flight from what was clearly a distressing scene had finally been checked and she was heading towards him. Not consciously. She hadn't seen him. She wasn't seeing anything except the floor stretching ahead of her.

'Your bag is in the car, sir,' the bellhop informed him.

He nodded, unable to tear his eyes away from the long beautiful legs of Sunny York, walking her towards him. The memory of her warm vibrancy played havoc with his usual cool decision-making processes. Here was opportunity. The guy at the blackjack table was one hell of a big loser and that loss was right in front of Bryce to be capitilised upon. The urge to do so was more compelling than any urge he'd had for a long time.

She was free.

He wasn't, Bryce sternly reminded himself. Kristen was wearing *his* ring. But not a wedding ring yet. And before he could have any further second thoughts, a fierce surge of highly male instincts moved him to intercept Sunny York's path to the exit doors.

'Miss York...'

Legs were planted in front of her—the legs of a big man—and that voice...her heart quivered as a weird certainty crashed through the daze of misery in her mind. Bryce Templar was addressing her. Bryce Templar!

Her feet faltered, hesitating over making a wild sidestep to escape him. Even blinking furiously, she couldn't hide the moisture in her eyes. Impossible to

face him...yet impossible not to. A man like Bryce
Templar would not be snubbed. Not by an employee
of his company.

'I was looking for you after the awards presentation,' he said purposefully.

It surprised her into raising her gaze to his. 'Looking for me?' His eyes were green, pouring out interest
in her, and despite her embarrassment, Sunny found
she couldn't look away.

He smiled. 'You impressed me very much this
morning.'

At the vivid memory of how he had impressed her,
heat whooshed up her neck and scorched her cheeks.
It reduced her to total speechlessness.

'You have a remarkable gift for selling,' he went
on.

Somehow she managed to get her mouth around,
'Thank you.'

'I wondered if I could interest you in a proposition.'

Like having a baby with me?

Sunny blushed even more furiously at that terribly
wayward thought. Her mind was hopelessly out of
control. Bryce Templar had to be talking about a business proposition, which was stunning in itself...the
big man thinking she had a special talent for sales.

'Were you on your way somewhere?' he asked.

Realising her gauche manner was probably putting
him off—*putting Bryce Templar off!*—Sunny tried
desperately to adjust to this totally unexpected situation.

'I...I was just going for a walk. Out of the hotel. We've been closeted inside all day...'

'Yes, of course,' he said understandingly. 'I'll walk with you. If you'll just excuse me a few moments while I rearrange my schedule...' He smiled again, showering her with warm approval. '...I would like to talk to you.'

She nodded, completely dumbstruck at the prospect of strolling down the street, accompanied by Bryce Templar. Her whole body started tingling as she watched him stride over to the concierge's desk. He was rearranging his schedule to be with *her!* It was incredible, world-shaking.

Green eyes...she hadn't been close enough to see their colour before. They gave his face an even more striking character. Or so it seemed to her.

She watched him command the concierge's attention. He would naturally command attention anywhere, Sunny thought, even without the weight of his name and position. His height, the breadth of his shoulders, the sheer physical authority of the man, drew the gaze of everyone around him.

For once in her life, Sunny had the uplifting feeling of her own tallness ceasing to be a burden that had to be bypassed in her reaching out to others. She was short enough to hold her head high next to Bryce Templar without diminishing his sense of stature in any shape or form. Not that her height would be of any concern to him—a man of his power—but it was a relief to her not to feel conscious of it.

He made some quick calls on a cell phone, then spoke again to the concierge. Sunny was grateful for the time to pull herself together. A business proposition, he'd said, which was what she should be focusing on instead of letting foolish personal responses to him turn her into a blithering idiot. She had a future to consider…a future without Derek.

Yet when Bryce Templar turned back to her, his green eyes targeted her with an intensity that didn't feel business-like at all. Sunny was instantly swamped with an acute awareness of being a woman, every feminine instinct she had positively zinging with the electric possibility that *he* found her worthy of mating with.

It blew her mind off any consideration of business. Her pulse was a wild drumbeat in her temples. Her stomach clenched at his approach. He stretched one arm out in a gathering-in gesture and some madness in her brain saw him naked and intent on claiming her. Then his other arm pointed to the exit doors and the crazy anticipation rocketing through her was countered by a blast of sanity.

A walk…

That was the sum of his invitation.

Somehow she pushed her shaky legs into walking.

Bryce Templar did not, in fact, touch her. A bellhop rushed to open the door. When they emerged from the hotel, the big man fell into step beside her and Sunny instinctively chose to turn right because he was on her left and bumping into him was unthinkable in her dreadfully hyped-up state with fantasies running riot.

'Have you enjoyed being in Las Vegas?'

It was a perfectly natural question but his voice

seemed to purr in her ear, heightening her awareness of him. Sunny kept her gaze trained straight ahead, not trusting herself to look at him and keep sensible. *Business, business, business,* she recited frantically.

'I haven't really had much time to explore the city,' she answered carefully. 'The conference has been pretty much full-on. Which is what we're here for,' she quickly added in case it sounded like a criticism. 'And I have learnt a lot.'

'You apply what you know extremely well,' he remarked admiringly.

She shrugged. 'I like giving our customers the best deal I can.'

'Well, you've certainly done an excellent job of serving Templar Resources.'

'I'm glad you think so.'

'Oh, I think you'd be an asset to anyone, Miss York. Or may I call you Sunny?'

'If you like,' she gabbled, trying not to read too much into his charming manner.

'It suits you. You project a warmth that makes everyone want to bask in it.'

He was projecting a warmth that was sending her dizzy. She was tempted to glance at him, to check the expression on his face, but didn't quite dare. It was difficult enough to remain reasonably sensible when she was so affected by his close presence. If he caught her looking at him and held her gaze, she might melt into a mindless heap.

'What do you wish to see on our walk?' he asked pleasantly.

She had no plan. Her only thought had been to get

out of the casino. 'I...I just wanted...more of a feel for the city...before I leave.'

'I suppose, in a way, you could call it a very romantic city...full of dreams.'

Shattered dreams if you're a loser.

The flash of Derek was unwelcome, bringing with it the empty feeling of no marriage and no babies to look forward to. But she could never accept Derek as a husband or the father of her children now. It was definitely for the best that she'd found out what she would have been getting in him.

'The re-creation of romantic cities in the newer hotels—Venice, Paris, New York. They're quite fantastic facsimiles of the real thing,' Bryce Templar remarked, continuing his *romance* comment. 'Have you had a look at them?'

Sunny struggled to get her mind back on track with his. 'The Venetian and Paris, yes. They're amazing.'

'Well, we're walking in the right direction to see New York, New York. The Excalibur and the Luxor are further on beyond it. Very striking with their Medieval and Egyptian architectural themes.'

Suddenly struck by his indulgence towards what he perceived as her wishes, Sunny began seriously wondering what he wanted with her. Here he was, strolling along the Boulevard, playing guide to her tourist...what was it leading to? They reached an intersection and had to stop for the traffic lights to change. Taking a deep breath, and steeling herself to cope with the nerve-shaking magnetism of the man, Sunny turned to face him.

'Your time must be valuable,' she stated, her eyes quickly searching his for a true response.

'Isn't everyone's?' he replied.

'Yes. But...' She floundered as he smiled, showing obvious pleasure in her company.

'You need to relax. So do I. Is there any reason we shouldn't relax together?'

'No,' she answered breathlessly, her pulse going haywire at the realisation he *was* attracted to her, man to woman attraction. No mistake. No flight of fancy. The spark of sexual connection was in his eyes—the keen interest, the desire to know more, the hunter's gleam that said she was worth pursuing and he meant to pursue.

'Good!' There was a wealth of satisfaction in that one simple word. He reached out and gently cupped her elbow. 'The lights have changed. Let's go with the flow.'

The flow Sunny felt had nothing to do with the stream of people crossing the street with them. She was barely aware of them. The hand lightly holding her arm had the mental force of a physical brand...like Bryce Templar was claiming possession of her, burning his ownership through the sleeve of her suit-coat and making her sizzle with possibilities she would not have believed in a few moments ago.

Bryce Templar...wanting *her*. She hadn't been completely crazy back in the hotel lobby. But what did it mean to him? Was it his habit to pluck a woman out of a crowd—someone he fancied—and just go after her? It probably was that easy for a man like him. What woman would refuse the chance to...?

Shock stopped that thought from reaching its natural conclusion. Fanciful lusting was one thing. Real flesh-and-blood lusting was something else. Did she want to be a one-night stand for Bryce Templar, finishing off his trip to Las Vegas—a bit of relaxation, satisfying a sexual urge? Surely that was all it could be. She was an Australian, on her way back to Sydney tomorrow. An easy goodbye.

'How would you feel about transferring to the U.S., Sunny?'

It startled her into a fast re-think. 'You mean...leave Sydney...for here?'

'Not here. Your base would be Los Angeles. Or New York. They hold our biggest operations.'

Business!

Was she hopelessly out of kilter, imagining the sexual stuff?

Totally confused, Sunny tried to come to grips with this new question. A career move...an upward career move...out of her own country.

'Would you find that too much of a wrench?' he asked quietly. 'I realise it's a big ask, particularly if you're close to your family.'

Her family...Sunny almost groaned as she envisaged telling her mother and sisters she'd broken her engagement to Derek. No wedding. No marriage. No babies. She'd been a failure as a woman in their eyes for years and there she'd be, proving it again. Almost thirty and couldn't find Mr. Right. Sympathy would be directed to her face, pity behind her back, and she'd hate every minute of it.

'I have my own life to lead,' she said on a surge of proud independence.

'No family?' he queried.

'I have two married sisters and my mother is very involved with her grandchildren. My father died some years ago. I'd be missed...and I'd miss them...' She flashed him a look of self-determination. '...but I would certainly consider an offer.'

Triumph glinted in his eyes. 'Then I'll make it as attractive as I can.'

Her heart jumped into another gallop. It wasn't her imagination. This was highly personal. And he wanted her on hand *for more than one night!*

'The package would include a generous travel allowance,' he assured her. 'Which will enable you to visit your family on a reasonably frequent basis.'

Behind her, music suddenly boomed out over loudspeakers. So dazed was Sunny by the revelation that Bryce Templar was very intent on getting her where he wanted her, she almost leapt out of her skin at the fanfare of trumpets, her head jerking around, half expecting to see a triumphal parade for the victory being planned in the green eyes.

'It's heralding the dance of the fountains at the Bellagio,' Bryce informed her. 'Come...it's worth seeing.'

His arm went around her waist, sweeping her with him and holding her protectively as he steered her through the crowd gathering along the sidewalk to enjoy the promised spectacle. He didn't push or shove. People simply gave way to him, standing back to let him and his companion through to a prime watching position against the Italian-style balustrade that edged the man-made lake in front of the Bellagio Hotel.

He stood half behind her, dropping his hand onto the balustrade on her far side to keep her encircled in the shelter of his arm, though no longer touching her. It was an extraordinary feeling—being protected and cared for by this big man. Sunny couldn't help revelling in it. She was so used to fending for herself, it was wonderful to wallow in the sense of being a woman whose man was looking after everything for her, ensuring her pleasure.

Except he wasn't actually *her man*. But could he be? In a very real sense? The very male solidity of the body so close to hers was real enough. So was her response to it. If she leaned back...made deliberate contact...what would happen?

Recognising the wanton recklessness in that temptation, Sunny held still, telling herself to wait for his moves. It ill behove her to instigate anything, especially when she wasn't in his social league. She'd made a fool of herself, believing she could share her life with Derek. How big a fool might she be, reading far too much between the lines of Bryce Templar's proposition?

A row of high water spouts started running right across the lake. Circles of fountains shot into the air. The music moved into the tune of 'Big Spender' and the high lines of water looped and swayed and bopped to the rhythm like a human chorus line, dancing to a choreography that required perfect timing.

It was an entrancing sight, yet the song being used

struck a raw place in Sunny, reminding her this city revolved around gambling and all the lavish glamour, luxury and service were designed to draw people into big spending. Derek could very well be ruining himself here. Though the responsibility for that lay squarely with him, no one else.

Would she be ruining her life, impulsively linking it to whatever Bryce Templar wanted?

A gamble, she thought. A big gamble on a big man. An absolutely magnificent man who made her feel…exceedingly primitive.

The fountains whooshed high in a fabulous finale, then seemed to bow before gracefully dropping back under the surface of the lake, their dance over.

'That was lovely,' Sunny breathed, and with her eyes still sparkling appreciatively, turned to look directly at the man who was fast infiltrating every aspect of her life. She realised instantly that his gaze had been fixed on her hair. It slid from the soft mass of waves to meet hers, transmitting a sensual simmering that caught what breath she had left in her throat. The rest of her words emerged as a husky whisper. 'Thank you for showing it to me.'

For one electrifying moment he looked at her mouth. The blast of raw desire she felt emanating from him scrambled her mind. Her lips remained slightly parted, quivering in wanton anticipation.

Then he dragged his gaze back to hers, locking onto it with searing force as he murmured, 'Your pleasure is my pleasure.'

Her breasts prickled. Her stomach clenched. A tremor of excitement ran down her thighs. Her only

conscious thought, rising out of the raging desire he
stirred was…

It *was* real…his wanting her…as real as her wanting him right back…and if she didn't take this gamble
she might be missing the experience of a lifetime.

CHAPTER FOUR

BRYCE only just managed to stop himself from kissing Sunny York right then and there. The desire to ravish the mouth she seemed to be offering him was totally rampant. Only a belated sense of where they were—on a public street with a crowd of tourists around them—gave him pause, and his brain seized the pause to flash a neon-bright danger signal.

He was out of control.

Even so the physical rebellion against the warning was sharp and intense. But being in control had ruled his life so long, his mind automatically equated that factor with success, and losing this woman with rash action at this point was unacceptable. She had been skittish up until now. Moving too fast might frighten her off. It wasn't smart to assume too much too soon, not when so much was hanging on the outcome of one night with her.

Dumping Kristen.

Marrying Sunny York.

Persuading her into a pregnancy she might not want.

It was a huge leap for him to take. How much bigger for her, without his cogent reasons firing the impulse to take this alternative road?

He stepped back, gesturing a continuation of their

stroll. 'A little slice of New York awaits you up ahead.'

Her beautiful amber eyes reflected inner confusion. Her vulnerability to what he was doing smote his conscience for a moment. She was afloat from her broken engagement, undoubtedly wanting an escape from the hurt to both heart and pride, and he was ruthlessly intent on drawing her into his net.

But he would look after her and give her a life full of riches if she came his way.

With that soothing justification riding on the advantage he knew he was taking, Bryce slid into charm mode, offering a whimsical little smile as he sought to ease her personal turmoil with outside interests.

'The Statue of Liberty, the Brooklyn Bridge, and the Empire State Building are somewhat scaled down since they're merely dressing up a hotel, but very recognisable,' he said encouragingly.

She gave her head a little shake, alerting Bryce even more forcefully to the danger of moving too fast. She'd have to be totally insensitive to miss the sexual signals he'd been giving out and he suspected she was all too aware of them, given the way she'd been evading looking at him and the tension emanating from her. Although part of that could have been the need to hide her distress over the guy she'd just broken with.

'Have you had any first-hand experience of New York?' he quickly asked, talking to re-establish a more comfortable connection for her.

'Yes, but only a few days' sightseeing.' She hesitated, her eyes scanning his uncertainly. 'Not...not business.'

'What was your impression of it?' he pressed, relieved when she stepped forward, indicating her willingness to go on with him.

'It had an exciting energy...the sense of a lot happening.' Her mouth curved into a musing smile. 'Extra-wide sidewalks. Hot dogs, with an amazing range of choices for spicing them up. Delicatessens with exotic food. Caramel apples...'

He laughed. 'You must really enjoy food.'

'Yes, I do.' Her smile turned lopsided. 'My sisters accuse me of having hollow legs.'

'That has to be envy.' Her incredibly sexy legs were an instant source of erotic fantasies.

'Oh, I doubt they envy me much...except not having to diet.'

'Then I hope you'll have dinner with me. I shall enjoy eating with a woman who likes food and doesn't see it as the enemy to be kept at bay.' He slanted her a teasing glance. 'You will eat more than lettuce leaves?'

She laughed. It was a delightful gurgle, spontaneous, warmly responsive. 'We can skip salad altogether if you like.'

'I take it that's a yes to dinner?'

She scooped in a big breath. 'Yes.'

Elation zoomed through him. He didn't care if this was some kind of emotional payback to the guy back in the casino, who clearly hadn't valued her enough. She was coming *his* way...plunging ahead with reckless disregard for caution.

After all, he triumphantly reasoned, what did she have to lose? His cynical side told him if it was pride driving her, he represented a top replacement in the lover stakes. What he was offering had to be all gain from her point of view—better prospects for her career, a transfer away from her erstwhile fiancé, and an enviable reason to remove herself from any criticism by her family with the CEO of Templar Resources taking a personal interest in her.

But falling into bed with him might not be on her agenda.

She might not see that as wise—in her position as his employee—or, indeed, desirable in a personal sense, given her very recent disillusionment with her fiancé. On the other hand, there was always *impulse*.

Bryce started planning a seduction scene as he continued chatting to her, building a rapport to bridge what *he* had in mind.

Sunny couldn't believe her luck. Dinner with Bryce Templar. Dinner for two. Beautiful man, beautiful food, beautiful wine—probably the finest champagne to celebrate her taking up his proposition. Except she didn't quite know what his proposition was, apart from its involving her transfer to the U.S. *And the personal element.*

A convulsive little shiver ran down her spine. Was sex on the side the pay-off for a big career promotion? She quickly shut her mind to that creepy-crawly thought. Bryce Templar *liked* her. She could tell from the way he was talking to her. He wasn't just making conversation. He was enjoying the to-and-fro, smiling, laughing, connecting on *all* levels.

He was clearly interested in her as a person—what level of education she'd had, the various positions she'd held, leading to her current one, everything she'd done with her life so far, her likes, dislikes. In fact, Sunny was so intoxicated by his charm, it took her a while to realise he was actually conducting an in-depth interview while they wandered along the boulevard.

This was a somewhat sobering thought. Though reassuring, as well. It had to mean he was seriously considering where she could best be used in the company business, and more importantly, he didn't seem at all put off by anything she'd said.

He wasn't touching her, either. From the moment he'd stepped back from that highly charged moment in front of the Bellagio Hotel, he'd made no physical contact with her. Plenty of exhilarating eye contact, but nothing physical. Perhaps he had stepped right back from sexual temptation, deciding an intimate liaison with her was inappropriate.

Which, of course it was, Sunny told herself. If she held his high esteem, well…that was something very positive. Yet she couldn't stop her gaze from surreptitiously wandering over him whenever he paused in his role of tourist guide, pointing things out to her.

The muscular breadth of his chest caught her eye as they lingered under the Statue of Liberty at New York, New York, watching the roller-coaster that looped around the hotel, its riders screaming their excitement. A woman would surely feel safe, held to all that strength, and as a father, he would easily be able to carry two or three children, clutched in his arms or perched on those shoulders.

Then his hand captivated her attention, directing her to look at the figure of the magician, Merlin, in the windows of one of the turrets forming the Medieval castle which was the Excalibur Hotel...a large strong hand, deeply tanned, long fingers, neatly buffed nails. To have such a hand holding her breast, stroking her...did it know how to be gentle? Was he a caring lover?

When they stood between the giant Sphinxes that flanked the great pyramid of the Luxor Hotel...he didn't look at all dwarfed by them...more like a powerful pharaoh of his time...a man astride the world he was born to...and what would spring from the loins of this king of kings?

Sunny had to take a stern grip on herself. Secretly lusting over Bryce Templar was bad enough. She had to stop thinking about babies, especially connected with him. Whatever the deal he had in mind for her, babies would most certainly not be part of it.

They took the pedestrian overpasses to cross the street to the other side of the boulevard. The second one led them into the vast MGM complex, and an Elvis Presley impersonator strutting ahead of them and revelling in the notice he drew, evoked a bubble of shared amusement.

'I've never understood that,' Sunny murmured.

'What?'

'Why people want to be someone else.'

'You never entertain a dream world?'

She blushed, guiltily conscious of her x-rated dreams about him. 'Not to the extent of actually copying another person.'

'You're content to be you.'

'I guess I think…this is *my* life, however imperfect it is.'

The twinkling green eyes intensified to a sharp probe. 'What would make it perfect?'

Sunny couldn't reveal that, not when her idea of perfection revolved around the man he was. She could feel her blush deepening and frantically sought some kind of all-purpose answer.

'I don't think we can expect perfection. Making the most of who we are is probably the best aim.'

'So a good career in your chosen field would satisfy you?'

Was he testing how long she might stay in his employ? She couldn't bring herself to lie. A career that interested her was great but it wasn't *everything*. 'Well…not completely,' she admitted, hoping he didn't need total dedication to her work. 'I think most of us would like to have a…a partner…to share things with.'

Surely he would, too. Being alone was…lonely. Though he probably never had to be alone if he didn't want to be. Here she was…providing him with company, simply because he chose to have it, and he hadn't even met her before today. Maybe he was self-sufficient enough not to need any more than a bit of congenial company whenever he cared to fit it in.

'What about children?' he asked, jolting her out of

her contemplation of what she wanted for herself, and hitting directly on a highly sensitive need.

'Children?' she echoed, unsure where this was leading.

'Do you see yourself as a mother some time in the future, or are babies a complication you don't want in your life?'

She sighed. It probably wasn't the smart answer but she simply couldn't pretend that missing out on having a family—at least one baby—wasn't any big deal to her.

'I would like to have a child one day...with the right father,' she added with a wry wistfulness.

'What would encompass *right* to you, Sunny?'

This was getting too close to the bone. Having envisaged *him* as the genetically ideal father, Sunny's comfort zone was being severely tested by his persistence on these points.

They had descended the staircase from the street overpass into the MGM casino area, and were now moving past a café with a jungle theme. Unfortunately Tarzan did not leap out and provide a distraction, and Bryce Templar's question was still hanging.

'What relevance does that have to my job?' she asked, deciding some challenge should be made on the grounds of purpose.

'It goes to character,' he answered smoothly. The green eyes locked onto hers, returning her challenge with an intimate undercurrent that flowed straight around her heart and squeezed it. 'I'm very particular about the character of anyone I bring into close association with me.'

Close.

The word pounded around her bloodstream, stirring up a buzz of sexual possibilities again.

'Some women's prime requirement of *right* would be a certain level of income. The child-price, one might say,' he said sardonically.

Sunny frowned. 'I could support a child myself. That's not the point.'

'What is?'

She rounded on him, not liking the cynical flavour of his comment, and hating the idea of him applying any shade of it to her. '*You* have a father. What was right for you as a child?'

His mouth curled with irony. 'For him to be there when I needed him.'

Which she could no longer trust Derek to do. The clanging casino noise around her drove that home again.

'You've just said it all, Mr. Templar,' she stated decisively.

Her eyes clashed with his, daring him to refute that this quality overrode everything else. It carried the acceptance of responsibility and commitment, displayed reliability and caring, and generated trust...all the things Derek had just demonstrated *wrong* about himself.

Bryce Templar didn't refute it. He stared back at her and the air between them sizzled with tense unspoken things. Sunny had the wild sense that he was scouring her soul for how *right* a mother she would be, judging on some scale which remained hidden to her but was vibrantly real in the context of mating.

'Let's make that Bryce,' he said quietly.

And she knew she had passed some critical test. They stood apart, yet she could feel him drawing her closer to the man he was, unleashing a magnetism that tugged on all that was female in her...deep primitive chords thrumming with anticipation.

He smiled...slowly, sensually, promisingly. 'You must be hungry by now. I am.'

'Yes,' she replied, almost mesmerised by the sensations he was evoking. She was hungry for so many, many things, and every day of this week in Las Vegas she had felt them slipping away from her, leaving an empty hole that even the most exciting career couldn't bridge. Maybe she was crazy, wanting this man to fill the emptiness so much, she was projecting her own desire onto him.

'This way,' he said, and proceeded to guide her around the casino area to the MGM reception desk.

Sunny was barely conscious of walking. She was moving with him, going with him, and he was taking her towards a *closer* togetherness. Dinner for two. On first-name terms. Sunny and Bryce.

She expected him to ask about restaurants at the desk, but he didn't.

'Bryce Templar,' he announced to the clerk. 'A suite has been booked for me.'

'Yes, Mr. Templar. The penthouse Patio Suite. Your luggage has been taken up. Your key?'

'Please.'

It was instantly produced. 'If there's anything else, sir...'

'Thank you. I'll call.'

He was steering Sunny towards the elevators before she recollected her stunned wits enough to say, 'I thought you were staying at the conference hotel.'

'I'd already checked out when I saw you in the lobby.'

She frowned, bewildered by this move. 'Couldn't you check in again?'

'I preferred to keep my business with you private.'

Private...in a private penthouse suite.

A penthouse for playboys?

The elevator doors opened and Bryce Templar swept her into the empty compartment...just the two of them...doors shutting off the crowded casino, closing them away from all the people who had surrounded them on their walk, and suddenly there was silence...except for the hum of the elevator and the thundering beat of Sunny's heart.

CHAPTER FIVE

SHE stood rigidly beside him. Bryce willed the elevator to go faster. He knew she had expected a public restaurant, not this, but he had to get her alone with him. Close the net. His mind worked double-time, producing a string of soothing words, ready to answer any protest she might make about the situation he'd set up.

He saw her hand clench. She took a deep breath. Her face turned to him, her stunning amber eyes swimming with questions. Her mouth moved, tremulous words slipping out. 'I don't think…'

'Don't think!'

The growled command came from nowhere. Before any sophisticated reasoning could stem the urge that exploded through him, Bryce scooped Sunny York into his embrace and kissed her with such devouring intensity, there was no possibility of any more words being uttered by either of them.

He was so hungry for her—for all that she was— the raging desire coursing through him directed all movement. The elevator stopped. The doors slid open. He swung his woman off her feet, hooking her legs over his arm, and it felt absolutely right as he carried her to his suite because her hands were linked around his neck and her breasts were pressed to his chest, and she was kissing him back as wildly as he was kissing her.

The slot-card in his hand opened the door. He kicked it shut. No bed in sight. The suite was a two-storey apartment. Catching sight of the staircase he charged up to the intimate rooms on the next level and straight into the bedroom. Seduction did not enter his head. There was no finesse at all in the need that had him put Sunny on her feet so he could get her clothes off. And his own.

He couldn't wait to have her naked with him, to feel every luscious curve of her, skin to skin, her lovely long legs in intimate entanglement around him. It excited him even more that she was as eager as he was to be rid of all barriers, her hands just as frantically busy with undressing, wanting to feel him and know everything there was to know.

Her eyes were a blaze of gold, burning him up. Her mouth was sensationally passionate in its hunger for his. Her hands were wildly erotic in their touch. Her glorious hair was pure sensual pleasure, its scent, its silky mass, its flashing colours. And fully naked, she was stunningly perfect, her whole body so lushly female, soft and supple, calling on him to perform as a man, and he was so ready to, the drive to take and possess was overwhelmingly immediate.

He laid her on the bed, kneeling over her for a moment, savouring the sight of her—all her sizzling warmth lying open to him, every inhibition abandoned in the sheer craving for this mating with him. Her arms lifted, winding around his neck, pulling him down, wanting him as much as he wanted her.

No foreplay. It wasn't needed by either of them. They were both poised for a completion that had to come. He drove forward, sheathing himself in her moist heat, revelling in her ecstatic welcome, loving the sense of being deep inside her. And her legs wrapped around him, holding him in, exulting in the sensation of feeling him there, then urging him to repeat the action, to move into the rhythm that would take them both on the upward climb to where they had to be…together.

It was an incredible feeling—this compulsive copulation with her—his intense arousal, the sense of being so aggressively male, primitively needful of having *this* woman. Somehow she embodied everything he had to have, and it drove him into a frenzy of possession.

The amazing, the wonderful, the totally exhilarating thing was, she was just as frenzied as he was in wanting what he was giving her, and when he could no longer stop himself from climaxing, she was right there with him, joining him in a fantastic meltdown that seemed to fuse them as one.

For a few moments he spread his body over hers, wanting to feel the whole imprint of her femininity as he kissed her again, sealing their oneness—all of him, all of her, together, as deeply and totally as they could be. The satisfaction of it was euphoric. He wished he could stay where he was, but it wasn't fair to subject her to his weight for long.

He rolled onto his side, scooping her with him to lie in the cradle of his arm, holding her snuggled close to him. He was swamped by a sense of tenderness for her, this woman who made him feel as a man should feel, wanted for what he was, not *who* he was...an instinctive, compulsive wanting.

His hands moved over her, gently caressing, loving the soft texture of her skin, soothing the endearing little tremors his stroking aroused. His fingers threaded through her hair, enjoying the winding spring of curls around them. The urge to bind her to him was so strong, he didn't even pause to wonder what she was thinking—or feeling—about what had happened between them. The words simply spilled straight out.

'Marry me!'

He didn't even realise he spoke in a command. Her head was resting just under his chin. He felt it jerk slightly, a startled little movement.

'What...' The question was choked with disbelief. He heard her sharply indrawn breath, then, '...what did you say?'

Bryce was not about to back off from having the advantage of their intimacy to press his suit. He rolled Sunny onto her back and propped himself up on his elbow beside her, meeting her stunned gaze with an intensity of purpose that was not to be shaken. He lightly traced the line of her full-lipped mouth with his finger as he delivered a clear and firm statement.

'I want you to marry me, Sunny York.'

Sunny could scarcely believe her ears. But he'd said it twice and his eyes were serious. Her sensitised lips were tingling and she couldn't get her mind thinking in any order at all. It didn't help when he lowered his head and grazed his mouth over hers, his tongue sliding seductively across the soft inner tissue, and the hand that had caressed her lips, moved down to cup her breast, gently kneading it as his thumb fanned her nipple with tantalising tenderness.

He knew how to do it right. Sunny's mind completely glazed over again, mesmerised by the rightness that had swamped it from the moment she had been seized by lustful madness in the elevator. He kissed her more deeply, re-igniting all the exciting sensations of previous kisses.

'I want you to be my wife,' he murmured against her lips, his breath still mingling with hers.

His wife.

Then he was trailing kisses down her throat, to the breast he hadn't touched yet, covering it with the hot excitement of his mouth, sucking it erotically, pumping pleasure through her in delicious spasms, building a craving for more and more.

'I want you to have my child,' he said, moving to her other breast, sliding his hand down to caress her stomach in circular sweeps, as his mouth played sweet havoc and her mind flashed images of...

His child.

His child in her womb, his child at her breast...the baby she'd love to have...with this man as the father...the man she'd secretly thought would be the *best* father.

And now he was kissing her stomach, as though he was imagining his baby in there, and his hand was between her thighs, stroking them apart, making room for him to come to her again, exciting the need to have him there. Such intense sensations of pleasure, demanding the fulfilment only he could bring, but when he moved again, it was to drive the need higher, his mouth closing over her sex, setting her on fire with the exquisite brushing of his tongue, the desire for him quickly reaching exploding point.

She heard herself cry out for him, begging, pleading, desperate for him to answer the ache inside her, and he responded immediately, filling her with a glorious rush of satisfaction as he plunged himself deeply into the quivering place that yearned for him.

It felt so good, so right, and she revelled in every stroke of him inside her, loving the hard fullness that kept pushing the pleasure of his possession higher and higher until she felt herself shattering around him, moving into a sea of bliss, and he rocked her there, bringing wave after wave of beautiful feelings that spread through her entire body. The spasms of euphoria kept coming even after he had climaxed and they were simply lying together, luxuriating in the intimate peace of needs fulfilled.

Feather-light fingers stroked the curve of her spine. His cheek rubbed over her hair. She felt his warm breath fan her temples as he spoke, gruffly demanding a reply from her. 'Say you'll marry me, Sunny.'

Marry him.

It was a huge step to take. Her still-floating mind struggled with the enormity of it, hardly believing it was real. It was still difficult to believe all she'd done with him was real. But here she was, lying naked on a bed with him, having been brought alive sexually to a fantastic extreme she had never imagined possible. Nevertheless, this...this hasty plunge into intimacy, did not warrant a hasty plunge into marriage!

'Bryce...'

She hadn't even called him by his first name before! The unfamiliarity of that alone had her hauling herself up to look at him, face to face...this man who seemed intent on marrying her...Bryce Templar, the CEO of Templar Resources, whom she had thought so far removed from her normal life, the idea of a marriage between them had been inconceivable.

His green eyes were simmering with pleasure in her. A sensual little smile curved his lips. 'You're even more beautiful with your hair all tousled,' he murmured.

He thought her *beautiful?* Her hair was probably a tangled mop with all the threshing around she'd done in the heat of passion. And that memory brought a flush to her face.

'We've barely met,' she rushed out, embarrassed by her terribly wanton behaviour.

'So?' He stroked her hot cheek, his eyes smiling reassurance. 'What has time got to do with anything? When something is right, it's right.'

The conviction in his voice eased her troubled sense of having acted out of character. This *was* different—what anybody could excuse as extraordinary circumstances.

'You might not feel it's so right tomorrow,' she said cautiously, still finding his proposal too stunning to really accept it could be genuine.

'Sunny, you said you wanted a partner. So do I, and *everything* about you feels right to me.' His eyes flashed absolute conviction as he added, 'And I don't believe you're the kind of woman who'd go to bed with a man *you* didn't feel right with.'

That was true. She'd never been promiscuous, and one-night stands were definitely not her scene. It was a relief to hear him reading her correctly. Although she'd never been hit by such overwhelming lust before. But lust wasn't love, more an instinctive thing running right out of control. She couldn't believe getting married should be based on *instinct*. There were many more factors involved in making a partnership work well.

'We're even in the same business,' he went on. 'All the more to share with each other, understanding what's involved in our lives.'

She'd thought she had that with Derek. It should be a plus in a relationship. But then she'd believed a lot of things about Derek—for months!—and only found out differently this past week. What seemed right could turn out very wrong indeed.

'And I want a child,' Bryce Templar pressed. 'A child who is wanted just as much by its mother. That's you, Sunny, isn't it? You want to be a mother.'

She couldn't deny it.

'We're not getting any younger,' he pointed out. 'How old are you?'

No harm in answering that question. 'Twenty-nine.'

'I'm thirty-four and I don't want to be an old father. The sooner we make a baby, the better.' He cocked a quizzical eyebrow. 'Any chance we might have already made one?'

It shocked her that protection had not entered either of their heads. Unsafe sex... 'I hope you're not a health risk,' she shot at him.

He laughed. 'No, I'm clean. And I have no doubt you are, too, Sunny York.'

She sighed her relief. 'Well, at least I'm on the pill.'

'Why not throw the pills away?' His eyes twinkled wickedly. 'We can try again. All night...'

Just like that? Plunge into pregnancy with him as the father? Her fantasy answered? Yet fantasies were one thing, realities quite another. People didn't make life commitments, virtually on the spur of the moment. She frowned at him, thinking that stopping contraception would be a very reckless decision, especially when she was feeling all at sea about what had already happened with him, let alone what he had in mind now.

'Do you really want that, Bryce?' she queried, uneasy with the way he seemed to be rushing decisions that shouldn't be hurried. It still sounded strange, using his first name, yet she could hardly call him Mr. Templar in this situation.

'Oh, yes,' he said decisively, a gleam of determination in his eyes. 'I wouldn't play you false about such serious things, Sunny. You're the woman I want as my wife, in every sense. Give me my way and we'll be married tomorrow.'

'Tomorrow!' She shook her head dazedly.

'Easily done in Las Vegas and I see no point in wasting time.'

'I'm on a flight home to Sydney in the morning.'

'You don't have to be on it. And I certainly don't want you on it. In fact...' He reached for the telephone on the bedside table. '...I'll make arrangements for your luggage to be packed and brought here.'

'Bryce!' she cried, grabbing his arm, totally rattled by how fast he was moving.

He shot her a piercing look. 'Do you *want* to go back to that hotel, Sunny?'

And break up what was happening here?

Run into Derek?

'No.' She withdrew her hand, fluttering a helpless gesture. 'It's just...'

'Leave it to me. I'll fix everything.' He grinned at her. 'How about running us a bath while I make the calls? I'll notify the Sydney manager that you're staying on and I'll get the hotel staff to pack everything for you and get it delivered here. Okay?'

Sunny took a deep breath.

It felt as though Bryce Templar was taking her on a wild roller-coaster ride and it was scary to think of where it would lead next, yet to get off...without knowing more...and the grin on his face made him *so* attractive, inviting her into his private and personal world, delighted to have her with him.

Besides, getting on the plane with Derek in the morning was not a happy prospect, seated next to him on the flight to L.A., then the long haul to Sydney. Arguments, stress, wondering what might have been if she'd stayed...

'Okay,' she echoed, the word torn out of her need to escape a miserable return to Sydney, as well as the strong temptation to stay right where she was with

Bryce Templar, at least long enough to see what the end of the ride might be like. 'But what about my ticket home if...'

'Do you imagine I wouldn't make good on that for you, should you want to go?' he cut in quietly.

Her heart cringed at her unwitting impugning of his integrity. 'I'm sorry. This is all so fast...'

'I promise I'll look after you. Whatever you need. Whatever you want. All you have to do is tell me, Sunny.'

She took another deep breath to steady her whirling mind. 'Okay. I'll stay on...for a while.'

His grin sparkled with triumph this time, putting a host of butterflies in her stomach. She had the wild sense that Bryce Templar had carried her into his cave and was now busily shutting off all exits until he had his way with her. Which clearly meant she needed some space to calm herself down and start thinking rationally about her immediate future with him.

'I'll go find the bathroom,' she said, remembering his suggestion of running a bath...*for both of them!*

'You do that,' he approved heartily, reaching for the telephone again. 'This won't take long.'

She slid off the bed, and very conscious of her naked state with his eyes watching her, headed straight for the most likely door to an adjoining bathroom. It proved to be precisely that and she shut it behind her to ensure at least a few moments' privacy.

As caves went, this was certainly a sumptuous one, Sunny couldn't help thinking as she noted the Italian marble accents, the positively decadent Roman tub, even a television set to watch while bathing. Life with

Bryce Templar could be very seductive with such luxuries. All the same, she was not going to be rushed into any rash decisions. The old saying—*marry in haste, repent at leisure*—was a good warning.

On the other hand, she might as well enjoy what was here. Having turned on the taps to fill the bath, she sprinkled in some scented grainy salts from a very elegant jar, then added a blue syrupy mixture that instantly frothed into bubbles. Satisfied that she wouldn't feel quite so naked with a mass of foam to hide behind, Sunny moved around the other facilities.

Beside the toilet was a European bidet—very civilised sophistication—and in a drawer of the vanity table she found a packet of hairpins which she proceeded to use, hoping not to get her hair wet in the bath. *Tousled* might look beautiful to Bryce but *wet* was definitely not her best look.

For a few moments she stared at her own face in the mirror. What did Bryce Templar see in her that he hadn't seen in the many many women who must have traipsed through his life? Why should he suddenly decide she was the one to marry?

She was passably attractive. Her eyes were probably her best feature. Her nose had that irritating tilt that always got sunburnt if she wasn't careful and her mouth was too wide. The hair he admired was the bane of her life. And she'd hated her legs in her teens, so long and gangly, though they did have more shape to them now she was older and her figure more mature.

Shaking her head, the puzzle of Bryce Templar's choice still unresolved in her mind, Sunny stepped over to the bath, which was now well filled. She turned off the taps and lowered herself gingerly into its warm foamy depths. A sigh of sheer pleasure relaxed the tension raised by too many uncertainties. Sinful pleasures, she thought, wondering if she would end up rueing her decision to stay.

A knock on the door preceded its being pushed slightly open. 'May I come in?' was courteously asked.

'Yes,' she answered, her heart jiggling nervously at the thought of sharing this bath with him. But since she'd already shared far more, it was way too late to start feeling shy.

The door swung wide open and Sunny's breath caught in her throat at the sight of him coming towards her. He had been naked on the bed, but she hadn't really seen him like this. They'd been too wrapped up in other things. His physique was stunningly male, magnificently proportioned and power-packed with just the right amount of masculine muscle.

He looked...fantastic.

And she could have *him* as her husband!

But there was more to marriage than the physical, Sunny hastily berated herself. This terribly strong desire he inspired was probably the most sinful pleasure of all.

'Brought the menus with me for us to choose dinner from,' he said with a smile, waving the large folders he held in his hand. 'I'm hoping your appetite will match mine. I think we should order a feast to celebrate our coming together.'

Dinner! She'd forgotten all about it.

'Yes. That would be good,' she agreed, trying to get her mind focused on an appetite for food instead of the very distracting appetite for him.

He laid one folder on the floor beside her, fetched a towel for her to dry her hands, then lowered himself into the bath, facing her from the other end. 'Your luggage should be here within the hour and I've let the Sydney people know you won't be on tomorrow's flight with them,' he tossed at her as he opened his menu to peruse its contents.

She wondered what reaction that announcement from Bryce Templar had caused amongst her colleagues. Had Derek been told? Her stomach suddenly clenched. What would Derek think? What would he do?

I don't care, she told herself on a surge of violent anger for the uncaring way he had treated her. She grabbed the towel, dried her hands, picked up the menu and opened it, determined on ordering a veritable feast.

The die was well and truly cast now.

One way or another, she'd thrown in her lot with Bryce Templar.

Dinner for two!

...the blue metal mask in confusion. Stony face
that projecting a round of insistent rejection.
Bryce looked, and acted with open view. I see
than we are before when ... and in this
objectivity, it.

CHAPTER SIX

BRYCE saw the belligerent tilt of her chin and her
mouth compressing into a line of determination as she
reached for the menu. He had no difficulty in reading
what those telltale expressions meant. The boats were
burnt. There was no way back. Not tonight nor tomorrow. No point in not making the most of her time
with him.

He smiled to himself. The net was closed. Not exactly how he'd meant to do it. In fact, he'd lost the
plot completely in his somewhat intemperate need to
have her, but he was now satisfied he hadn't hurt his
end purpose by it. He may well have improved his
chances of convincing her to marry him. Mutual desire was a strong persuader. And he had the rest of
the night to capitalise on it.

He moved his legs to lie in tandem with hers, enjoying the long silky slide of her calves and thighs.
She was certainly built perfectly for him. The way
they fitted together was especially satisfying. He
looked forward to much more of it.

'What are your favourite foods?' he asked, wanting
eye contact with her.

Her lashes slowly lifted. From this distance the col-
our of her eyes looked darker, more a warm brown.
They still lit up her face. She had a wonderful face.
Not classically beautiful, like Kristen's, but Kristen's

was like a smooth mask in comparison. Sunny's was alive, projecting a wealth of fascinating expression.

'I *love* lobster,' she stated with open fervour. 'I see they've got Maine lobster on the menu, so I'm definitely having that.'

He laughed at the rich satisfaction in her voice. She truly was a delight in every sense. He would enjoy having her as his wife. 'What else?' he prompted.

She listed everything she found tempting, displaying a relish for food that whetted his own appetite. He couldn't remember ever having such fun, discussing a menu. They were discussing the merits of a selection of sweets when the telephone rang, interrupting the pleasurable anticipation of a superb meal.

'Probably announcing the arrival of your luggage,' Bryce commented, hauling himself out of the bath to deal with the call since the telephone, although in the bathroom, was out of his reach and he didn't want Sunny answering it.

She laughed at the foam flaking off him as he moved. 'You make a great snowstorm.'

'Maybe we should have the Bombe Alaska for sweets,' he tossed at her, grinning as he snatched up a towel.

'No. I really fancy the raspberry soufflé.'

'It'll probably sink before it gets here. Think about it.'

Her eyes chided him. 'Spoilsport.'

He laughed, loving the natural interplay between them. Sunny was much more relaxed with him now, not on guard at all. Which had to bring her closer to what he wanted.

Having wiped his hands, he picked up the receiver, expecting a quick communication. 'Templar here.'

'Ah, Mr. Templar. Miss York's luggage has arrived. And so has a Mr. Derek Marsden, demanding to see Miss York. He claims she is his fiancée.'

'No way,' Bryce returned tersely.

'He is being very insistent, sir. One could say threatening, if you take my meaning.'

Bryce tensed, a savage aggression instantly gripping him. The last thing he needed was Sunny's ex-fiancé hanging around, creating scenes, and possibly swaying Sunny off the course she had chosen. He had to protect the ground he'd won.

'I'll come down and deal with it. Give me a few minutes.'

'Thank you, sir. I'll hold the gentleman here. Should I send the luggage up?'

'No. Not yet. I'll deal with that, too.'

'As you wish, sir.'

He slammed the receiver down, startling Sunny. 'Something wrong?' she asked, wide-eyed at his change of mood.

He grimaced an apology. 'A business problem.'

'Not my luggage?'

'Still coming,' he answered, quickly towelling himself dry. 'I have to go and meet an associate in the lobby, Sunny. It should only take ten minutes or so. While I'm gone, call room service and order what we've decided upon.' He forced a smile to put her at ease with the situation. 'You get to choose the selection of sweets. Okay?'

She caught the undercurrent of urgency. 'Is it a bad problem?'

'No.' He relaxed his face into a wry expression. 'Just vexing that it's come up when I'd rather be with you.'

She smiled. 'Then I'll try not to miss you.'

'Think of great food,' he teased, and was off, striding for the bedroom and the clothes he had to put on before facing the rival he had to dismiss.

He couldn't allow this Derek Marsden any room for worming his way back into Sunny's affections. Bryce frowned, wondering how Marsden had picked up on where she was. He hadn't given out that information.

He dressed at lightning speed, his mind ticking over possibilities. Marsden had arrived at the same time as Sunny's luggage. Possibly he had gone to her hotel room, found her clothes and toiletries being packed by staff, then followed the trail, greasing palms with big tips to learn what was going on.

Dog in the manger stuff, Bryce decided. If Marsden had really valued Sunny, she wouldn't be here in this suite. No doubt it was *his name* being involved that was sticking in Marsden's craw. In any case, he had no claim on her. She had given him back his ring. The break was clear-cut and Bryce aimed to keep it that way. No second chance for Marsden.

Sunny was still in the bathroom, happily ignorant of her ex-fiancé's intrusion on the scene. Hoping to make his absence as brief as possible, Bryce made a fast exit from the suite, summoned the elevator, and waited impatiently for its arrival. His mind skated through his impression of the man he'd seen at the blackjack table this afternoon—about the same height as Sunny, fairish hair, clean-cut type of college-man looks, lean build.

Physically, Bryce knew he was the far more intimidating man. He didn't expect a fist-fight, but Marsden could turn ugly, faced with the frustration of losing out. The trick was to get him to accept defeat, and if possible, allow him some dignified retreat.

The elevator arrived. The descent to the lobby was uninterrupted. Bryce spotted Marsden near the reception desk but proceeded there without giving any sign of recognition. They had never personally met and Bryce had no intention of displaying any knowledge of him. He directed an inquiring gaze to the clerk who had handled his check-in.

Marsden stepped forward before an introduction was made. 'Mr. Templar,' he called aggressively.

Bryce paused, raising a challenging eyebrow at the man accosting him. His suit was crumpled, his eyes bloodshot, and he was clearly the worse for having imbibed too much alcohol. Possibly a belligerent drunk.

'I'm Derek Marsden,' he announced. 'Of the Sydney branch of Templar Resources.'

'Indeed?' Bryce returned frostily. 'I understand you're causing a problem here. What concern do you have?'

He rocked back on his heels, glaring at Bryce. 'I want to see Sunny.' His hand lifted, pointing an accusing finger. 'I know she's here. I know she's with you. And you have no right to stop me from seeing her. She's my fiancée.'

'Miss York is certainly with me,' Bryce acknowledged. 'We are negotiating her transfer to a new position in Los Angeles. As to her being your fiancée, Miss York has declared herself free of commitments and she is certainly not wearing an engagement ring.'

He flushed. 'We had an argument. She took it off. That's what I want to see her about. Fix it all up again.'

'Then I'd be obliged if you'd try doing so in your own time, Marsden. Not mine. This is a business meeting and you are interrupting without invitation.'

'So what is her luggage doing here if it's business?' he jeered, turning nasty.

'It was brought here at Miss York's request,' Bryce replied, keeping a cool calm. 'I understand she does not wish to return to the conference hotel. Perhaps you are the reason why, Marsden.'

The edge of contempt stung him into defence. 'I just want to talk to her. Get things straight. She's gone off half-cocked if she's discussing a transfer and that won't do *you* any good when she comes to her senses.'

'Miss York has presented herself to me as a free agent and I see no reason to give you the opportunity to harrass her. She is at liberty to contact you if she so wishes. Now if you'll excuse me...'

Bryce started to turn away.

'She's mine!' came the seething claim as Marsden grabbed him by the arm.

Bryce squared his shoulders and cast a quailing

look at the slighter man. 'You work for Templar Resources, Marsden?' he said quietly, threat embodied in every word.

The angry glaze in the bleary blue eyes wavered.

'You are not doing yourself any favours here,' Bryce continued quietly. 'I suggest you return to your hotel, sleep off this...unwise burst of aggression...and catch your flight back to Sydney in the morning...where you may still have a job.'

The hand dropped away.

Marsden stood slack-jawed, not having foreseen these consequences.

Bryce had no compunction whatsoever in using the power of his position to get this man out of Sunny's life. He signalled the concierge who instantly hurried over. 'Please get Mr. Marsden a taxi and see him into it,' he instructed and nodded towards a couple of security guards who could assist if necessary. 'Put the fare on my tab.'

'I'll pay for it myself,' Marsden blurted out in fierce resentment.

Bryce subjected him to one more icy look. 'As you wish. Goodnight, Marsden. I hope you have a safe trip home.'

He shouldered past the concierge and marched off towards the exit doors. Bryce watched him out, not quite sure he'd read the man correctly. Australians had a reputation for bucking authority, going their own way. Still, he'd given Marsden something to think about and he hoped it was enough to make him realise there was no chance of a reconciliation with Sunny.

He moved over to the clerk he'd dealt with at the reception desk. 'The bellhop can bring up Miss York's luggage now. If there's any more trouble from Mr. Marsden, let me know.'

'Certainly, Mr. Templar.'

He shared the elevator with the bellhop. Sunny's luggage comprised a medium-sized suitcase and a standard carry-on, obviously an economic travelling wardrobe, enough to suit what was required for a conference with its various functions, but not enough for a prolonged stay. Some shopping would need to be done.

He dismissed the bellhop at the door to the suite, carrying in the luggage himself. Seeing no sign of Sunny in the living room, he took the bags upstairs, expecting to find her there. She was not in the bedroom. Nor the bathroom. The yellow suit was gone from where it had been dropped on the floor. So were her other garments.

Bryce stared at the empty space that was no longer littered with her clothes. Unfamiliar feelings—fear, panic, an intolerable sense of loss—started screwing him up inside. His mind literally jammed over the thought she had gone…left him…was even now on her way back to Derek Marsden. He should not have given her any time alone to reconsider what she was doing.

Or maybe he was jumping the gun.

He hadn't searched the entire penthouse.

With his heart pounding harder than if he'd run a marathon, Bryce made a fast sweep through the other

upstairs rooms. Nothing! No sign of her presence anywhere!

'Sunny!' he roared as he reached the staircase and
started down it.

'Yes?'

He stopped dead, his head swivelling to her voice.
She was there, standing in the opened doorway to the
outside patio. Her hair spilled in glorious disarray
around the huge collar of an oversized white bathrobe. She hadn't dressed. Her feet were bare.

For several moments they stared at each other. It
hit Bryce that she looked very vulnerable, caught in
a time-warp between the past and the future, not
knowing quite where she was or what she was doing
here. He was her only focus right now.

Was he being fair to her?

Would she take Marsden back if the guy cleaned
up his act and grovelled enough?

'Is everything all right?' she asked, seeking guid-
ance.

'Yes,' he asserted, determination sweeping back.
He'd be a better husband for her than Marsden.
'Everything settled,' he assured her, walking down
the rest of the stairs. 'I took your bags up. They came
when I was in the lobby.'

'Thank you.' She looked discomforted by that information, half turning back to the patio as she added,
'I was out looking at the view. All the neon lights
along *The Strip*...'

'You're the best sight of all, Sunny,' he said
warmly, crossing the living room to reach her. 'I was

just thinking how much I'd like to come home to you every night. Exactly like this.'

Her gaze veered back to his and he caught the sense she wanted to believe him, but was uncertain of filling that role. He smiled, wanting to convince her of his pleasure in her. It was no lie.

'Did you get onto room service and order our dinner?'

She smiled back. 'I did. And I hope you're really hungry, Bryce.'

'I am.'

For you.

And that was no lie, either.

He drew her into his embrace. Her eyes were liquid amber, silently, eloquently asking if this was right, or was she hopelessly astray in being here with him.

He kissed her to burn away the doubt.

There was no doubt in his mind.

He wanted her as his wife and she was going to be his wife. Whatever he had to do to win her, he'd do.

CHAPTER SEVEN

SUNNY woke slowly, savouring the sense of a warm delicious languor...before she remembered why her body felt so replete and relaxed. A little electric jolt went through her brain. She sucked in a deep breath and carefully, quietly turned her head.

Her breath whooshed out on a relieved sigh. She didn't have to face him yet. The rest of the bed was empty. He'd obviously wakened before her and left her to sleep on. She resettled herself and started thinking.

Bryce Templar...

Her hand drifted over her naked body...remembering. He was certainly a fantastic lover. She closed her eyes, recapturing the incredible sensations in her mind, the power of them, the intensity of the pleasure that had rolled on and on through so much of the night.

What time was it?

Her head jerked up, eyes flying open again. The clock-radio on the bedside table read 9:14. The flight she should have been on from Las Vegas to Los Angeles had already left. Panic galloped through her heart, stirring up the enormity of what she had done...cutting herself off from all she had known...Derek...

She struggled to get a grip on herself. It wasn't all

irreversible. She could still go home if she wanted to. Bryce had promised that decision was hers anytime she chose. As for Derek...

She dropped her head back onto the pillow. Unaccountably tears pricked her eyes. Derek hadn't even tried to change her mind when she'd handed him back her ring. All those months of planning to marry...and they'd had many good times together. Her family had liked him. She had really believed they would make a good marriage together.

But he hadn't even tried to get her back.

He could have tracked her to the MGM hotel if he'd wanted to. Gambling had obviously meant more to him than she did. And always would, now that he'd caught the bug for it, Sunny savagely reasoned. Her chin set with determination. She would not mourn his passing out of her life.

Which left her with...Bryce Templar.

And his proposal of marriage.

She heaved a huge sigh. He was definitely a marvellous lover but she couldn't marry him on that basis alone, however tempting it might be. As it was, plunging into this intimacy with him was probably going to complicate any career decisions she made. Nothing was clear-cut anymore.

But...he certainly made her feel good about herself. For him to desire her so much...to want her as his wife... It was quite mind-boggling.

How could *he* make up his mind so fast? Wasn't he taking a big risk in committing himself to a marriage with a woman he'd only known for a day? Not even a full day! Surely a man in his position should take more care in choosing a life partner.

Not that there was anything wrong with her, Sunny quickly reasoned, but how could he know that? On such short acquaintance? Was he so confident of reading her character correctly? Maybe that was a skill CEOs had to have—choosing the right people for the right positions.

Deciding that lying here by herself wouldn't give her any answers, Sunny rolled out of bed and headed for the bathroom. She took a quick shower, all the time wondering what Bryce was doing downstairs—reading the newspaper, making business calls, having breakfast, *waiting for her?*

Grateful to have her own toiletries, she brushed her teeth, applied a light make-up, and did what she could to get her hair in reasonable order without taking too much time with it. She hesitated over dressing, not knowing what plans Bryce might have. Easier just to wrap herself in the bathrobe until some decisions were made.

She heard Bryce speaking to someone as she started down the stairs and paused, not wanting to interrupt anything important.

'Just do your best to keep the cost to a minimum.'

It was a terse command, showing impatience with the caller.

'No, I won't change my mind.'

Even more terse. Whoever was on the phone to him was stirring Bryce's ire and whatever was put to him now evoked an icy reply.

'Understand me very clearly, Sherman. It's finished. We simply write this off. No more negotiation. Nothing—absolutely nothing—will get me to reconsider this decision. Now you take it from there, knowing my position on this is irreversible.'

The cut-off click created a pool of silence that seemed to echo with the ruthlessness with which Bryce had ended the deal that had been in negotiation. Someone had pushed too far, Sunny thought. All the same, it was an insight into the character of the man. He wielded command with an iron fist when the occasion demanded it.

She couldn't imagine him ever being seduced by gambling. He would make a limit and stick to it. Yet he was gambling on her with his proposal of marriage, wasn't he? Perhaps that, too, had a limit. He'd give so much time to her, then...

Shaking off the thought which only time could prove right or wrong, Sunny proceeded down the stairs. Bryce was pacing back and forth across the living room, a frown of deep concentration on his face. Then, either hearing her soft footsteps or sensing her presence, he stopped, his face clearing as his gaze zeroed in on her.

'Ah! Some morning sunshine!' he said warmly. 'You slept well?'

'Very well.' He was wearing his bathrobe, too, so Sunny didn't feel uncomfortable about not being dressed. 'Have you been up long?'

He shrugged. 'There were a few things I wanted to get out of the way so I could concentrate entirely on you.'

His eyes were eating her up and Sunny's heart was

doing cartwheels. It was so incredibly flattering to be desired by him, and she couldn't help remembering how magnificent he was, under that bathrobe.

'All done?' she asked, trying to sound matter-of-fact.

'All done.' He grinned as he swept her into his embrace, his eyes teasing her caution. 'So here it is—the next morning—and I still want to marry you, Sunny York.'

'Mmm…have you had breakfast?'

He laughed. 'I was waiting for you.' His mouth grazed over hers with tantalising sensuality. 'And you taste so good,' he murmured.

'Food is good, too,' she choked out, struggling to keep her mind clear of the seductive web he was weaving again.

'Then we shall order breakfast right now.'

Everything she wanted, when she wanted it… It was terribly difficult to keep her head on straight around Bryce. He swamped her with such tempting attractions, most of all himself.

Over a sumptuous breakfast, she finally managed to focus on addressing the question of business. 'We haven't settled on the kind of position you're offering me, Bryce.'

'First and foremost, the position of my wife,' he answered, his eyes unmistakably reflecting very determined purpose.

Sunny's heart skipped a beat. 'What if I say no to that?'

'You haven't said no yet. Until you do, Sunny, I'll

be doing everything within my power to persuade you to say yes.'

She could feel his power winding around her and wondered if it would prove irresistible in the end. 'I really don't know much about you, Bryce,' she stated defensively.

'What do you need to know?'

His heart, she thought, then doubted her own ability to judge that, given her terrible misreading of Derek's heart. Needing to start somewhere, she said, 'Well, I know you have a father. What about the rest of your family?'

'My mother died when I was three. I was her only child.'

No wonder he'd counted so much on his father being there for him! 'I'm sorry. That must have been hard...to be left without a mother,' she said with sincere sympathy.

His mouth twisted with irony. 'Oh, my father kept trying to provide me with mothers. He married four more times, resulting in four divorces. I have a half-brother and two half-sisters, but their respective mothers took their children with them. I was...am...the only constant in my father's life as far as family is concerned. We are...very attached to each other.'

'I see,' she murmured, thinking his father hadn't exactly set an example on how to make a marriage work.

'Do you see that I don't want an easy-come, easy-go marriage?' he countered as though he could read her thoughts. 'That I want a wife who is as committed to me and our children, as I would be to her?' he pressed on. 'Parents together, Sunny. A stable home.'

All that he felt he hadn't had himself? It was strong motivation, but was motivation enough when faced with a clash of needs? Sunny suspected Bryce was very used to getting his own way on most things.

His eyes glittered knowingly as he added, 'You've come from a stable home, haven't you? It means something to you.'

'Yes. It's why I don't want to rush into such a serious step as marriage.'

'What reservations do you have about me?'

Sunny frowned, not having any criticisms to make except... 'I don't understand why you're so keen, so quickly.'

Her eyes flicked to his in sharp challenge, determined on getting a reply that satisfied her sense of reality—a reality that was not wrapped in hothouse passion or persuasive patter.

He leaned back in his chair but it was not a move that held relaxation, more putting a weighing distance between them as he considered what answer to give her. She could almost feel the wheels clicking around in his mind, and there was no mistaking the tension emanating from him as he came to a decision.

'I'll tell you why, Sunny,' he said quietly, and she tensed, every intuitive instinct telling her that something important was about to be revealed, and he was counting on her understanding, counting on a positive response from her, as well.

'My father has a heart condition. Every day he lives is a medical miracle. For some time he has been agitating for me to marry, have a child. I know this is a symptom of his own rather immediate sense of his mortality, but it is his dearest wish and I would like to give him that sense of our bloodline going on before he dies.'

A bloodline! It sounded almost Medieval. Like feudal lords securing a succession. 'You want to marry me for your father's sake?' she asked incredulously.

'No. I could have married any number of women for my father's sake. I am considered...' His mouth took on a cynical curl. '...very eligible in the marriage stakes.'

Sunny did not doubt that truth.

'But I didn't want just any woman as my wife, Sunny. I wanted a woman who felt right to me. A true partner on many levels.' His eyes blazed with conviction. 'Every instinct I have is shouting that I've found her in you.'

Her heart jiggled with an intemperate burst of joy. It took a tremendous effort to override the wild response and keep boring in on her misgivings. 'You trust your instincts so much?'

'In every aspect, you shine with rightness. No other woman ever has. Not to me.'

'Then I'll still be right to you in a month's time,' she argued.

'And my father might be dead in a month's time.'

It was softly said, yet it hit Sunny hard, making her remember her own father's death. He'd been a volunteer fire-fighter, supervising a burn-off. The wind changed unexpectedly, trapping him and two others. No goodbyes. No chance to tell him how much he'd given her and what it had meant. Not even a few moments to show him she loved him.

Bryce leaned across the table and took her hand in his, pressing his sense of urgency, his *caring*. 'I want to marry you now, Sunny. Today. And present you to my father as my wife for him to see what I see...so he won't fret about the future anymore.'

What she saw was how much it meant to him to answer his father's need, and she remembered him saying his father had always *been there for him*.

She understood the urgency he felt, and was moved by his reasoning, honoured that he had chosen her to be the wife he took home to his father, yet she could not get over the uneasy sense of being an instrument to resolve a situation, rather than a woman who was loved for herself.

It was difficult, knowing where Bryce was coming from, to set his proposal aside. The impulse to give him what he wanted was strong. She'd always wanted a marriage based on the kind of values she believed in, and in a way, Bryce *was* offering that—solid family values—yet...

'I'm sorry. I...I need to think about this.' Her eyes eloquently pleaded his patience. 'I can't do it today, Bryce. I can't just...walk straight into it.'

He brushed his thumb over the back of her hand, as though wishing—willing—to get under her skin. 'What's troubling you most, Sunny?' he asked quietly, his eyes meeting her plea with a caring concern that stirred more emotional confusion.

She shook her head, thinking she was probably being a fool, putting what had proved to be an illusion with Derek over the substance Bryce probably represented.

'Tell me,' he softly pressed.

'I always thought I'd get married for love,' she blurted out. 'Not…not for convenience.'

'Convenience,' he repeated with a harsh edge, frowning over the accusation implied in it. 'If I'd wanted convenience…' He bit off the thought, shaking his head. His gaze flashed to hers, searing in its intensity. 'I swear to you this marriage is not a convenience to me, Sunny. I want you. I want you in my life. How can I make that more clear to you?'

'It's too fast!' she cried. 'It's just too fast!' She pulled away from him, pushing up from the table in her agitation, gesturing a helpless apology. 'You've made it clear and I…I know this must be frustrating to you, but…I need time to feel sure I'm doing the right thing for me, too. I'm sorry…'

'It's okay,' he quickly assured her, rising from the table and holding out his hands in an open gesture of giving. 'I didn't mean to make you feel pressured. I guess my own decision is so clear-cut to me…' He grimaced an apology. 'I'm not about to force you into marriage, Sunny. It has to be your choice, too, and if you're not ready to make it…'

'I'm not. Not yet,' she quickly added, acutely aware she didn't want to shut the door on his proposal, however many doubts were clouding it for her.

'Then we'll make other plans for today,' he offered, smiling to soothe her agitation. 'Simply spend time together. Are you happy to go along with that?'

She nodded, her chest feeling too constricted to

find breath for more words. He was the most stunningly attractive man she'd ever met and one side of her was clamouring it was madness not to accept him on face value alone. Only the painful thud in her heart argued that *want* wasn't love, and she craved real love from the man she married—the kind of love that lasted a lifetime.

'Have you seen the Grand Canyon?'

'No,' she whispered shakily.

'Would you enjoy a ground/air combination tour—a helicopter flight, as well as travelling around the rim by road, hiking where you want to?'

Sunny scooped in a quick breath. 'Yes. I'd like that very much.' Outside distraction…more time…

'Shall I book it for an hour's time? Can you be ready to go that soon?'

She nodded, grateful to seize on quick action. 'It won't take me long to get dressed. I'll start now.'

Eager to be on the move, she was already heading for the staircase when he paused her with the words…

'One last thing, Sunny…'

'Yes?'

He had stepped over to the telephone table and had picked up the receiver to make the booking. His head was cocked quizzically and she was anticipating a further question about the trip they had agreed upon.

'You said…*married for love*. What, in your mind, is love?'

Her mind went completely blank, then tripped into a welter of needs that Derek's defection had wounded, very badly. Out of the miserable emptiness of bitter disillusionment came the one thing love had most represented to her, and precisely what Derek had torn away.

'Emotional security,' she said, with all the passion of having been stripped of it.

'I see,' he murmured, as though weighing her answer against what he could balance it with.

'What is love to you, Bryce?' she shot at him, wanting him to feel some of the vulnerability he had stirred with his question, though she couldn't really imagine him feeling insecure about anything.

He seemed to consider his answer carefully before giving it, perhaps gearing it to her own. She didn't want that. She intinctively shied from thinking he would pursue his purpose relentlessly, calculating every word, every move.

'I think it's something that grows,' he said slowly, his eyes holding hers with hypnotic intensity. 'It begins with strong mutual attraction, and is fed by the caring each person demonstrates towards the other. It's a commitment to caring, and without that commitment it dies a quick death.'

Derek, she thought, not caring enough for her.

While Bryce...how much did he care? His answer sounded genuine, a deeply held personal belief, not a reply designed to win her over.

His mouth quirked into an appealing little smile. 'A fair assessment?'

'Fair enough,' she agreed. 'I'll think about it.'

He nodded and turned away to make telephone contact for the tour booking.

He cared a lot about his father, Sunny thought, and

as she continued on upstairs, she decided he would
care a lot about any child he fathered, too.

But how much for her?

Would love grow between them?

Could she take that gamble?

CHAPTER EIGHT

BRYCE clamped down on his impatience. Rushing Sunny was not going to work. Marsden had obviously caused too much emotional damage for her to trust easily. Yet he was quite certain her instincts sided with him. She would never have responded as she had without feeling the same deep attraction he felt.

Or was it rebound stuff—an overwhelming need to be desired?

That was one need he could certainly answer. Desire was simmering through him right now as they waited for the arrival of the elevator to take them down to the limousine which would transport them to the helicopter base. The stretch jeans and T-shirt Sunny had pulled on showed every delectable line and curve of her. She'd crammed one of the conference caps over her rioting curls, and it, too, seemed provocative on her, like a perky invitation to whip it off and free her hair.

Free everything!

The elevator doors slid open. Sunny glanced nervously at him as she stepped into the empty compartment. Bryce's chest tightened as he followed and hit the control panel for the ground floor. What good was restraint? Pouncing on her the last time they had been in this elevator together had propelled them into an intimacy that was working for him. Why should he hold back now?

The doors closed.

Driven once more by the urge to claim her as his, Bryce reached out and wrapped her in his embrace. Her lovely amber eyes lit with alarm. 'No pressure,' he gruffly promised, lifting a hand to gently stroke the tension from her face. 'I just have a need to feel you with me.'

The amber softened into a golden glow as he bent his head to kiss her and there was no hint of resistance when his mouth touched hers. The hands that had rested warily on his shoulders, slid quickly to link around his neck, an eager signal of her desire to feel him with her, too.

It was more than enough to push Bryce into seeking all she would give him and her active response as he deepened the kiss instantly ignited a passionate drive to break the emotional barriers in her mind, to draw all her feelings towards him with such dominant force, nothing else existed for her but the two of them together.

He pressed her closer, exulting in the long, feminine legs clinging to his, the soft fullness of her breasts spreading across the hard muscle of his chest, the whole delicious pliancy of her body as it seemed to crave every contact with his. He was so strongly aroused, so exhilarated by the fervour of her response, he wasn't aware of the elevator having come to a halt at ground level.

The whirr of the doors opening did belatedly register in his consciousness, but by the time he'd lifted his mouth from Sunny's, the doors were closing again, which was fine by him. He didn't want to stop what he was doing. They could ride straight back up to his suite and...

'Bryce...' An urgent gasp.

'Mmm?'

'We're down!'

He sighed, swiftly deciding he had regained some ground with her and playing for more might be a bad idea. He swung aside, reached out and pressed the Open Doors button just as the elevator was being sealed shut again.

Her hands dropped from his neck as she turned to face the exit, but she made no move to distance herself from the arm he'd left around her waist. They stepped out to the lobby together, which was a far more satisfying situation to Bryce than the apartness she'd been subtly maintaining since their breakfast conversation. It was clear he had to keep stoking this very mutual desire and sweeping her along with him until she accepted he was the man for her.

'You slut!'

The ugly words sliced through Bryce's pleasurable mission-plan, and the sight of Derek Marsden advancing on them switched his mind to red alert! Beside him he felt Sunny's whole body jerk with shock and her feet came to an abrupt halt, which halted him, as well, since no way was he about to let go of her.

'Derek?'

The name spilled from Sunny's lips, even as her mind recoiled from the horrible name he had called her. The shock of seeing him was stunning enough, having expected him to fly out on the plane to Los Angeles, but to be so insultingly labelled in public...

'Yeah,' he jeered. 'Thought you'd neatly got rid of me, didn't you? Sneaky bitch!'

'That's more than enough!' Bryce rapped out in a steely voice.

Sunny felt the surge of aggressive tension whipping through him, his hand on her waist gripping harder, pulling her protectively closer.

'She's taking you for a ride, Templar,' Derek threw at him, his eyes shooting daggers. 'Want to see the ring she gave back to me yesterday so she could go after you?'

'That's not true, Derek!' Sunny cried, appalled by this attack on her integrity.

He ignored her, plucking the engagement ring out of his shirt pocket, holding it in his clenched fist with the diamond pointing at Bryce, shaking it at him as he poured out more venom. 'No doubt you can buy one bigger than this.'

'That has nothing to do with why I broke with you, Derek, and you know it!' Sunny fiercely protested.

He turned on her in vicious accusation. 'You left me and went straight off with him.'

Sunny shook her head, bewildered by the totally unfair interpretation of the situation.

'At my instigation,' Bryce sliced in. 'You are mistaken. It was I who approached Miss York, not the other way around.'

'Miss York...huh!' Derek snorted derisively.

'Think I didn't see you in a clinch in the elevator just now?'

'I have asked her to marry me,' Bryce stated with icy dignity.

'*Marry* you?' Sheer fury twisted Derek's face. 'Well, let me tell you she was marrying *me* this time yesterday.' His eyes blazed at Sunny. 'What did you do? Give him the eye all the time you were sitting in the front row of the conference room?'

'No! I didn't do anything!' she cried, flushing with the guilt of having nursed lustful thoughts. But only in a fantasy way, not aimed to draw Bryce's attention to her.

'Like hell you didn't!' came the bitter rebuttal. 'You got your eye on the main chance and goodbye Derek.'

The sheer injustice of his slurs on her character whipped up Sunny's fury. 'It was goodbye Derek because all you could think about was gambling!'

'Well, it's you who's gambling now, you scheming little gold-digger! And I hope Templar sees you for what you are before he's fool enough to marry you.'

'I am not a gold-digger! It's you who wanted easy money.'

'At least I earn what I spend. I don't trade in sex for it.'

'Oh! Oh!' Sunny gasped, reduced to speechlessness.

'That is too offensive!' Bryce growled, his whole body clenching, ready to spring.

But it wasn't his fight, Sunny thought frantically. It was hers. And she had to fight back.

'Offensive!' Derek hurled at Bryce, too aroused to be intimidated. 'I track her here and discover there's no room in the name of Sunny York. She spent the night with you, sleeping her way to the top. That's *offensive*.'

'You're right!' Sunny snapped, leaping in to defend herself. 'I did sleep with him. *He* found me more attractive than a roulette wheel.'

'Well, you just keep spinning for him. I don't want a whore as my wife.'

'You insult Sunny once more and I'll ram the words down your throat,' Bryce bit out, violence shimmering in the air.

'No!' Sunny instantly swung towards him, slamming a hand on his chest, desperate to prevent any movement towards Derek who was shaping up to slug it out.

Fists wouldn't resolve anything. It would only make the whole scene uglier and more public than it already was.

She glared at her ex-fiancé over her shoulder. 'We have nothing more to say to each other. Please go, Derek.'

He glowered at Bryce to prove he wasn't intimidated, then sliced a look of contempt at Sunny. 'Screw you! I'll have plenty to say to everyone else about why you ditched me.'

'You keep your filthy mouth shut or I'll shut it for you,' Bryce threatened, his chest swelling against Sunny's hand.

'You don't have that much power, sucker!' Derek challenged, and on that jeering note, turned his back on both of them and strutted off as though he was cock-of-the-walk.

'Don't do anything, Bryce,' Sunny pleaded, frightened by the aggressive jut of his chin and the fighting strength that was teetering on the edge of exploding.

His gaze lowered reluctantly to hers, eyes glittering. 'You want me to let him get away with that slimy slander?' he demanded, rage clipping every word.

'It's true I broke my engagement to him yesterday,' she said, trying to excuse some of the offence.

'And none too soon,' Bryce ground out. 'There was no *love* for you in that outburst, Sunny.'

No...no love...just wounded ego and vile nastiness. Her stomach felt sick with it. 'Did you believe...' She anxiously scanned the glittering green eyes. 'Did you believe anything of what he said about me?'

The question brought a beetling frown. 'You know I don't. How could I? I've been with you every step we've taken together.'

But her staying with him as she had *was* open to misinterpretation. 'You don't think I'm a...a golddigger? Out for what I can get?'

'Not you, Sunny,' he declared with ringing certainty.

She felt intensely grateful for his belief in her. Into her distressed mind flashed the image of Bryce always standing by her, ready to defend, to protect, caring with the kind of strength Derek had never had.

'Do you still want to marry me?' she asked.

'You think *he* could change what I feel?' came the incredulous challenge.

'No. Not you,' she answered, somehow knowing that very deeply. Bryce Templar trod his own path, and suddenly she wanted very much to share that path with him. It looked safe. It looked secure.

He cupped her face in his hands, commanding her full attention as his eyes blazed into hers. 'I want you, Sunny York. I'd marry you right this minute if I could.'

The warmth of his skin took away the dead coldness left by Derek's emotional kicks in the face. Bryce's desire for her sizzled into her bloodstream, bringing a vibrancy that re-energised her whole body.

'Then I will…I will marry you, Bryce,' she heard herself say, as though the words were drawn from a place she was barely conscious of, yet she knew even as she said them, she wouldn't take them back.

Bryce knew instantly it was a rebound decision. Her eyes were focused on him but they had a calm, almost distant expression in them, not one sparkle of happiness or even warm pleasure in the thought of being his wife. He should have felt an exhilarating zing of triumph, having achieved his goal so quickly, but the achievement wasn't his. It was Marsden's. Nevertheless, the prize was there to take, and Bryce was not about to let it slip away.

'Today?' he pressed.

'Yes.' Her mouth quivered into a challenging little smile. 'Right this minute if you like.'

He grinned, determined on being cheerful. 'We do have to get a wedding licence first.'

'Is that a problem?'

'A quick trip to the courthouse. No problem at all.'

'Then let's do it.'

As simple as that! Except Bryce was acutely aware of the complex undercurrents to this apparent simplicity. As he linked Sunny's arm around his and steered her out of the hotel to the waiting limousine, he asked himself if it was wise to take advantage of a decision she may well think better of, given a few hours' distance from Marsden's backlash.

Which reminded him that Marsden had to be dealt with before he caused more damage. He'd call Sherman as soon as he had a free minute. His crafty lawyer could speak to Marsden in L.A., pound home enough unpleasant legalities to demonstrate that silence held the greater good.

'Mr. Templar and Miss York,' the chauffeur greeted them affably, holding the passenger door open. 'Lovely day for a trip to the Grand Canyon.'

Bryce paused, hit by an unaccustomed sense of wrongness. It was a rare moment of indecision for him, yet this choice did involve Sunny very intimately and he did not want her to be unhappy as his wife. He lightly squeezed the hand resting passively on his arm, drawing her gaze to his and watching intently for any hesitation on her part.

'Are you sure about marrying me, Sunny?'

'Yes, I'm sure,' she stated decisively.

'You don't want to go to the Grand Canyon and take some time to think it over?'

'No.' Her chin was set in determination. 'I want to marry you today.' Her eyes sparked into vehement life. 'If it's right for you, it's right for me!'

It snapped Bryce straight into positive action. He turned to the chauffeur. 'Use your car phone to cancel the tour and take us straight to the courthouse.'

'Yes, sir.'

Bryce handed Sunny into the limousine and followed to settle beside her.

'The courthouse,' the chauffeur repeated, grinning happily at the change of plan as he closed the door.

It has to be right, Bryce fiercely told himself, taking Sunny's hand and lacing their fingers in a grip of togetherness.

I'll make it right.

CHAPTER NINE

SUNNY was amazed how easy it was to get a wedding licence. All she had to do was produce her passport, fill out a form and sign her name. No wonder Las Vegas was called the marriage capital of the world, she wryly reflected. Here it was a totally hassle-free procedure—no other certificates required, absolute minimal red tape, no enforced waiting time.

Her mind quickly flitted over that last consideration. Waiting was not good in this case. Bryce's father wanted to see him married. Not that Will Templar would actually be at the ceremony, but the *fait accompli* would ease his mind and hopefully be beneficial to his heart condition. And then...no waiting any longer to have a baby. No more waiting at all.

As they emerged from the courthouse, the licence safely tucked in Sunny's handbag, Bryce took out his cell phone and made a call, asking to speak to a wedding consultant. Sunny frowned at him, not wanting any delay, not wanting some hypocritical fuss, either. This was a straight-out marriage of convenience, not a love affair to be celebrated in the traditional way.

'Don't we just go to one of the wedding chapels?' she said bruskly, much preferring to get it over and done with.

He shook his head, determination flashing from his

eyes as he answered, 'We do it right. Down to every detail.'

Sunny listened incredulously as he spoke to the consultant, listing off the kind of detail she would have thought important...if she'd gone ahead and married Derek. But that would have taken months of planning and scheduling and decision-making—chapel, flowers, kind of ceremony, photographer. Bryce was taking it upon himself to organise the whole wedding deal in a matter of minutes, *without even consulting her!*

Sunny burned with resentment. Wasn't her consent enough for him? Why did he have to make a production out of a wedding based on mutual purpose?

Having completed the call to his satisfaction, he put the phone away, tucked her arm around his and grinned, clearly delighted with his planning. 'Next stop,' he said, hurrying her towards the waiting limousine.

'What stop?' she demanded to know, beginning to feel truculent.

He addressed the chauffeur who was once again holding the door open for them. 'The Top of the Town Bridal Boutique.'

'A bridal boutique!' Sunny gasped.

Bryce bundled her into the limousine, still grinning from ear to ear. 'Going to get you the wedding dress of your dreams.'

'It's not necessary,' she gritted out, rebellion stirring.

'Yes, it is.'

'There's just the two of us getting married,' she

argued, turning to face him, to hammer home the truth as she saw it. 'It's not as if we're doing it in front of a whole pile of guests.'

It wiped the grin off his face. With a far more serious expression, he quietly asked, 'Aren't we the most important two, Sunny?'

Somehow that point steadied the angry whirl of protest in her mind. 'Yes, we are,' she conceded, though this was not the wedding of her dreams and she didn't want to pretend it was.

'Do you want to look back on our wedding and think of it as some hole-and-corner ceremony?'

She frowned, not having thought of what they were doing in *those terms*. 'It...it means the same,' she argued, still feeling out of step with his grand plan.

His green eyes seemed to glow like emerald fire as he softly said, 'I want my bride feeling beautiful, and knowing she is beautiful to me.'

Sunny's heart turned over.

'And I want you to be proud of the photos of our wedding when you show them to our children—their mother and father on the day they were married.'

Their children? They swirled in the mists of Sunny's imagination—a little boy and girl, examining their parents' wedding photos.

'We owe it to ourselves and them to do it right, Sunny,' Bryce pressed.

She hadn't been looking ahead. The blind need for positive action had seized her, and nothing else had really entered the equation. Selfishly blind, Sunny suddenly realised. This was Bryce's wedding, too.

And the intent of their marriage was to have a child...children.

As he said, love could grow out of caring for each other. He wanted her to feel like a beautiful bride, and why shouldn't she? She would have wanted that with Derek, and Bryce was better husband material than Derek had ever been.

She could send a wedding photo to her family. That would make her marriage to Bryce more right for them, as well. And shift any nasty cracks from Derek into the sour grapes category. A *fait accompli* would certainly help to put a stop to criticism.

'Okay. We'll go for all the trimmings,' she agreed, glad now that he had thought of them for her. 'But I pay for my own wedding gown, Bryce.'

He laughed. 'One last stroke of independence?'

It was more a matter of pride. 'I'm not coming to you on a free ride.'

He instantly sobered, his eyes flashing darkly. 'Wipe that guy and everything he said out of your mind, Sunny. This is our day. I know what you're worth to me and in that context, counting money is meaningless. I'm not buying you.'

Shame wormed around inside her, raising a flood of heat to her cheeks. 'I'm sorry, Bryce. I...I guess that really stung me.'

'Let it go,' he advised quietly. 'Don't let it spoil what we can have together.'

'I won't,' she promised fervently, her eyes begging his forgiveness. It was Derek who had humiliated her, not this man. Bryce made her feel good about herself.

He smiled, chasing the painful shadows of Derek away.

She smiled back, determined that she *would* feel beautiful as his bride. And she wouldn't count the cost of anything because that was how Bryce wanted it. Pleasing her husband-to-be was important.

When they arrived at the bridal boutique, he instantly commandeered a saleslady, instructing her to show Miss York the very best stock she had, and he expected to see the selection of gowns paraded in front of him so he could judge for himself which one most suited her very unique style of beauty. He then settled himself on a white satin sofa and waved them on to the business of looking at what was available.

'Now there is a guy I could really take to,' the saleslady remarked to Sunny, rolling her eyes in maxi-appreciation. 'You sure have won yourself a prize in him.'

'Yes. Yes, I have,' Sunny agreed, determined to believe it.

'Hmm...' The woman eyed her up and down. 'With your height and legs, we certainly don't want a crinoline-style skirt. Too much. Slim and elegant with a fabulous train, I'd say. Shall we start with that?'

Sunny nodded. 'Sounds good.'

'Perhaps something off the shoulder to frame that gorgeous mass of hair.'

Sunny barely stopped herself from rolling her own eyes at this description of her unruly mop. Reminding herself that Bryce liked her hair, just as it was, she simply said, 'Let's see.'

Maybe because it all seemed rather unreal, it was actually fun, parading the gowns for Bryce, striking poses for his studied opinion. His running commentary on the detail of everything made her laugh and he scored each showing out of ten. Oddly enough, his scores matched her own judgment, demonstrating like minds, which also helped to push any misgivings about her decision aside.

The fifth gown, however, brought the sense of fun to an abrupt halt. It wasn't exactly a *traditional* bridal dress, not silk nor satin nor even white, and it didn't have a train, either. But Sunny loved it and to her eye it looked perfect on her, nothing to be fixed or altered. It also made her feel more...*female*...than anything she'd ever worn before.

This time she didn't prance out of the dressing-room to show it off to Bryce. She walked self-consciously, knowing the slinky ankle-length gown in cream garter lace was moulded to her every curve. The long sheer sleeves added an elegant grace and the scooped neckline was just low enough to reveal the uppermost swell of her breasts. The image of a sexy swan floated into her mind and she couldn't help thinking this was how she would have wanted to look—to feel—if she was marrying for love.

Bryce was not alone on the sofa. Another man had joined him, apparently showing off the contents of an attaché case. They both turned to look at her. Bryce's face instantly lit up with pleasure.

'That one!' he said, almost on a note of awe, his eyes drinking in the whole lovely flow of it on her.

It mightn't be love but the blaze of desire in his

eyes was warming. Sunny slowly twirled around to give him the benefit of every angle, basking in the heat of his approval and the sexual response he stirred in her…needing to take the chill off her heart.

'Ten out of ten?' she asked.

'About ten thousand out of ten!'

'Good! Then I'll buy it.'

'You do that,' he fervently approved. 'But first come and have your finger sized for the wedding ring so our jeweler here can get moving on it.'

A wedding ring! A convulsive little shiver ran down Sunny's spine. This wasn't a game of fantasy dress-ups. They really were doing this…getting married!

It only took a few moments to get her finger sized. Then she was swept into choosing a bouquet from a book of photographs. There were so many pictures, they became a blur to her. When a bridal nosegay was suggested as the ideal accompaniment to her dress—complimenting it rather than distracting from it, Sunny simply let herself be guided.

It was also suggested that a pretty coronet of flowers matching those in the bouquet, would look better than a veil. Sunny instantly agreed. No veil. Somehow a veil was going too far, a mockery of what a wedding should stand for. Not even for her future children would she wear a veil. She simply couldn't bear it…Bryce lifting it off her face as though she were a true bride.

No!

She would pledge herself to him bare-faced.

Let there be at least that honesty between them.

With everything decided upon, delivery to the hotel was promised within the hour.

Back at the hotel, Bryce had lined up a hairdresser, a beautician and a manicurist to give Sunny every bit of pampering a bride could possibly want. Although the whole process felt more and more like a charade, since it all took place in their suite, it was easy enough to submit to it.

Trays of tempting finger food were brought to her, meant to satisfy any hunger pangs. Champagne was served. Sunny forced herself to nibble a few delicacies since fainting at the altar was hardly a good start to any marriage. The champagne was a good nerve-soother, but she was careful only to sip it occasionally. Being a drunk bride wasn't a good start, either.

The whirl of activity centred on her kept Sunny from thinking too much. She had to make more choices about her fingernails, her hair, her make-up, how the coronet of flowers was to sit. Only when all the preparations had been completed, and a fully dressed and meticulously groomed bride looked back at her from the mirror, did her nerves stage a revolt against any possible soothing. They plunged straight into an agitated tangle.

All the helpers had retired from setting the scene. The show was about to go on, except it wasn't a show. It was real, and the lines she would speak—the vows she would take—would affect the rest of her life.

'You take my breath away.'

Bryce...standing in the doorway...shaking his head as though she were a miracle he couldn't quite believe in. He took her breath away, too, looking utterly superb in a formal grey morning suit, a touch of cream in his silk cravat and a cream boutonniere to match the exquisite little flowers in her bouquet.

'Time for our photo call in the chapel studio,' he said huskily, pushing forward to collect her and take her with him.

Sunny took a deep breath and turned towards him, managing a somewhat shaky smile as she said, 'I'm ready.'

'Not quite.' His smile was a warm caress, driving off the rush of goose bumps on her skin. He took her left hand and slowly slid a magnificent emerald ring onto her third finger. 'I chose this for you. I hope you like it.'

'Bryce...' She could barely choke out his name.

Not a bigger diamond than Derek's. An emerald...and she felt his green eyes burning into her heart, willing her to take it without question, and wear it because it was *his* gift to her, *his* promise which would not be shabbily broken as Derek's had.

She swallowed hard to remove the constricting lump in her throat. 'It's...it's wonderful. Thank you.'

He wrapped his hand around hers and heaved a satisfied sigh. 'Let's go and get married.'

The final act.

Somehow his ring and his hand sealed it for Sunny. The decision was made...the outcome inevitable.

The half-hour photographic session in the chapel studio seemed to pass in a matter of minutes. Bryce was there with her every second, showing his pleasure in her, making her feel beautiful, making her feel...*loved.*

And the brilliance of the ring he'd placed on her finger kept dazzling her whenever she rested her hand on his chest or shoulder or next to her bouquet...a pear-shaped emerald—almost a heart—its vivid green hue emphasised by a border of white diamonds set in yellow gold. She had never seen anything like it...so very special, unique...and he'd chosen it for *her.*

For Bryce to value her so much...*she did want to marry him!*

It felt right.

They moved on to the chapel.

It was decorated with sumptuous floral arrangements.

A pianist sat at a grand piano, playing Celine Dion's song—'I've Finally Found Someone.'

A marriage celebrant smilingly beckoned them forward.

Somehow it didn't matter that the chairs on either side of the aisle were empty. Sunny thought fleetingly of her mother and sisters, but they had had their weddings. This was hers and Bryce's, and it belonged to them, no one else.

The civil ceremony performed was a simple one. There was no sermon, no gushy sentiments. To Sunny, the words seemed all the more meaningful for their straightforward simplicity.

When Bryce spoke his vows, his gaze remained steadfast on hers, and his voice carried a quiet solemnity that seemed to seep into her soul, spreading a sense of peace and dispelling any worries about a future with him.

She spoke hers just as solemnly, meaning every word of her commitment to him and their marriage. It was very real now. There was no going back from this moment. They would go forward together and make the best of whatever life served out to them.

Bryce had bought two gold wedding rings, one for her, one for him. It touched her that he wanted to display the fact that he was married—a bachelor no more—a husband who cared about his commitment to her.

'With this ring, I thee wed...'

He had to take off the emerald ring to slide the gold band into place, but the removal was only momentary. Sunny stared down at the dual rings on her finger, fitting perfectly, brightly shining proof that she now belonged to him.

'I now pronounce you husband and wife.'

Such fateful words...

Sunny poured all her hope for a good future with Bryce into the kiss that followed, and from him flowed a fervent eagerness to get on with it.

The wedding certificate was filled out, placed in a special holder, and given to Sunny—a lasting memento of a momentous day. The pianist was playing 'All The Way' as they thanked the marriage celebrant and the official witnesses.

They turned as a wedded couple to walk back down the aisle, and the words of the song were running through Sunny's mind, echoing what she hoped would prove true. At least she wasn't carrying any false illusions about this marriage. It was a matter of making it right, not expecting it to just turn out that way without having to work at it.

'Where is the Bryce Templar wedding?' a woman's voice shrieked, blowing the music right out of Sunny's ears.

Her step faltered as Bryce squeezed her hand hard, having come to a halt himself. Not only was tension ripping through him but any trace of a benign expression was gone, replaced by grim anger.

'Too late? Just finishing?' the woman's voice shrilled, then broke into furious determination. 'We'll see about that!'

Sunny jerked her gaze from the startling reaction from Bryce, just in time to see the woman burst through the entrance to the chapel, charging at battle pace before coming to a heaving halt at the start of the aisle, her gaze ripping Sunny up and down, then stabbing at Bryce.

'How could you?' she screamed at him.

The wild intrusion and the ear-piercing outrage was a total show-stopper. Sunny could only stare at the woman in a tumult of confusion. Who was she and why was she on the attack?

'How could you do this to me?' the woman demanded fiercely of Bryce, apparently deciding to ignore the bride beside him as though Sunny were nothing.

'Very easily, Kristen,' Bryce answered coldly.

Kristen? He knew her, then? It wasn't some complete madwoman on the loose?

'You ruthless, callous pig!' came the blistering indictment. Her face screwed into vicious fury. 'You'll pay for this!'

'Oh, I expect to,' Bryce drawled, a fine edge of contempt in every word. 'But not as much as I would have paid...*had I married you.*'

CHAPTER TEN

MARRIED!

Bryce had been going to marry *this woman?*

Even as Sunny's mind jammed with shock, her eyes swiftly took in everything there was to take in about his first choice—very, very classy with her polished blond hair falling in smooth perfection to her shoulders and cut to feather inwards from her ears to her throat, a stylishly artful frame for a face that was classic model material.

So was her body, though she wasn't quite as tall, nor as long-legged as Sunny. In fact, she was much better proportioned, her figure looking very sexy in a straw linen wrap-around dress and lots of gold accessories—chain belt, sandals, bag, bangles, necklace—all shouting the kind of money Sunny had never had at her disposal.

Bryce's contemptuous comment had acted like a smack on the face, but the jolt of it only lasted a few seconds. The pent-up fury was unleashed again, propelling the woman forward, her arm upraised to deliver a very physical slap to Bryce's face.

He caught her wrist before violent contact was made, holding it in a vice-like grip. 'Back off, Kristen!' he commanded in his steely voice, lowering her arm and slowly releasing it as he emphatically asserted, 'It's over. I told you it was finished this morning.'

This morning? Sunny glanced sharply at Bryce. Before or after she had agreed to marry him? There was a very disturbing question of integrity here.

He sensed her glance, caught the worry in it, and instantly answered, 'Before you woke up, Sunny.'

Even so, he had gone to bed with her first. Had he been testing her out before giving up Kristen?

'Damn you, Bryce!' his ex-fiancée stormed. 'I would have backed down if you'd given me the chance.'

'No chance.' He released Sunny's hand to put his arm around her shoulders in a very possessive and reassuring hug. 'I now have the wife I want.'

'A bargain basement bride, no doubt,' Kristen jeered, switching her gaze to Sunny, her grey eyes blazing scorn. 'You didn't even have the sense to marry him in the State of California.'

Which totally bewildered Sunny. What did California have to do with getting married?

'I'm sure it's beyond your comprehension, Kristen,' Bryce bit out coldly, 'but Sunny didn't marry me with an eye to a divorce settlement. Nor did she put a price on having a child.'

Money? Was that the currency of marriage in California?

'Then more fool her, with your record of using women as you please. Sucked her right in, did you, Bryce?' Kristen mocked savagely.

Sunny's mind whirled around this hasty marriage in Nevada—all Bryce's doing...except for her consent...which he'd started working for as soon as he'd had sex with her!

'I think women tend to draw from men what they put out themselves,' Bryce commented coldly. 'Users do get used, Kristen. It so happens Sunny is a different breed to you.'

'And such a convenient windfall *for you,*' she flashed back at him. 'Except this cheap move of yours is going to cost you, Bryce. Cost you big!'

A *windfall*...Derek's blow-up...her hasty consent...

'Go ahead and sue me, Kristen. Buying you out of my life will be worth every cent I have to pay.'

She bared her teeth, hissing, 'I'll take you down for as much as I can.'

'Your demonstration of greed in the prenuptial agreement leaves me in no doubt you'll money-grub as far as you can.'

Sunny's mind boggled over a prenuptial agreement. She'd always thought such things horribly cynical with their implication that the marriage commitment was inevitably a transitory thing and a division of property had to be worked out beforehand. If Bryce had even mentioned one, she would have backed off so fast...yes, she was a different breed. A *convenient windfall?*

'It's a straight breach of promise,' Kristen argued in fierce resentment, again sneering at Sunny as she added, 'throwing me over for her.'

'Oh, I think any judge would find good reason for that,' Bryce drawled, hugging Sunny even closer. 'My wife is such a warm contrast to you, Kristen...'

'I'm a Parrish!' she declared with belligerent arrogance. 'That name *means* something. I'll be listened to, Bryce Templar!'

'Yes, you undoubtedly will be,' he agreed uncaringly. 'The media will gobble up every bit of it as you prove you've been badly done by, revealing your avaricious little soul to the whole world in a public courtroom. You think you'll win their sympathy?'

Angry heat speared across her cheekbones. 'So...you figure you've got all the angles covered so you can cheat me.'

The words were flying so fast and furiously, Sunny was only catching the fact that Kristen was a gold-digger. Big time! Despite the name she set such store by.

'No agreement was reached, Kristen,' Bryce stated bitingly. 'You weren't content with what was offered.'

'What about *this agreement?*' She thrust her left hand up in a clenched fist, showing off the huge diamond ring on her engagement finger. '*It* shows something.'

'Yes. It shows my good will, which you proceeded to flout.'

She tossed her head defiantly. 'Well, don't think you're getting it back!'

'I don't want it back. I don't want anything remotely associated with you. We have nothing left to say to each other.'

'Except through our lawyers!'

'Agreed. Now if you don't mind...'

Sunny was subjected to a scathing look. 'Congratulations! You've got yourself a cold, calculating pig and you're welcome to him!'

Having delivered her best exit line, Kristen Parrish flounced a quick about-turn and strode out of the chapel, her stiff back eloquently denying any wounds whatsoever.

Just like Derek, Sunny couldn't help thinking. Rejection was never a palatable situation, but rejection in favour of someone else...that could definitely bring out the worst in some people.

Both she and Bryce had been badly misled in choosing their first partners for marriage. The question was...had they made the right choice now?

Sunny hoped so. With all her heart she hoped so. Yet she couldn't shake the feeling they had both been driven into this choice by a rebound effect...Bryce seemed to be everything Derek wasn't...and she was a *warm contrast* to Kristen Parrish.

A windfall marriage...

She shivered.

Bryce's arm instantly tightened around her. 'I'm sorry you were subjected to that, Sunny,' he said ruefully. 'My big mistake...'

She sighed, lifting her gaze to his in anxious query. 'Am I a windfall, Bryce?'

'Yes.' His eyes simmered with hot possessiveness. 'The best windfall that's ever come my way and I consider myself the luckiest man alive to have you as my wife, Sunny.'

Instead of Kristen, she thought.

'And I need, very much, to be alone with you,' he added softly.

He drew her with him, out of the chapel, into the elevator, back to their suite, and while Sunny took comfort from his desire for her, she couldn't stop the questions whirling around in her mind.

When had he calculated the difference between her and Kristen?

When had he decided to marry her instead?

And the bottom line—marrying to please his father—was she simply a better candidate? A cheaper candidate? *The bargain basement bride?*

CHAPTER ELEVEN

THE moment they were in their suite with the rest of the world shut out, Bryce turned her into his embrace. Sunny didn't mean to stiffen up, but she couldn't quite feel right, pretending nothing had happened to colour things differently. Her hands pressed nervously against Bryce's chest, holding her bouquet between them, her heart thumping painfully instead of happily.

'It's worrying you, isn't it...all that Kristen said?' Bryce quietly probed.

'Not...not all of it.' She fiddled with his boutonniere, wishing Kristen hadn't turned up. But there was no joy in hiding her head in the sand, now that she was more aware of circumstances.

'Tell me what's preying on your mind, Sunny. Let me fix it.'

'You didn't tell me about her.'

'She was irrelevant to us.'

No, she wasn't irrelevant, Sunny thought, and such a ruthless wipe-out of a woman he'd planned to marry—without any second chance offered—did not sit well with her. It was too...too uncaring.

'You were still engaged to her until this morning,' she reminded him, shying away from Kristen's accusation of him being a cold, calculating pig, yet calculation had to have come into his actions, given his need for a wife and the time pressure involved. To give up Kristen before he had secured Sunny's consent…had he? Had he really?

'Technically I was still engaged to her, yes,' he answered. 'In my heart, no.'

'In your heart, Bryce?' She lifted her eyes to scan his, to see how much he meant by that.

'When I asked you to marry me last night, *you* had completely obliterated any possibility of my ever marrying Kristen. I could never have gone back to her after you, Sunny.'

He looked and sounded genuinely sincere.

His grimace held a wealth of distaste as he added, 'I called Kristen at seven o'clock this morning, making it absolutely clear that everything was ended.'

She frowned, remembering similar words he'd spoken much later. 'I heard you talking on the phone to someone just as I was coming downstairs.'

'My lawyer. He had to be notified.'

'Because of the…the prenuptial agreement?'

'Yes.'

'Why did you do that with her? Was it the only way for you to get a wife and child…to buy them?'

His mouth twisted in a fleeting expression of bitter self-mockery. Then his whole face seemed to harden, his eyes reflecting a deep inner cynicism as he replied, 'Prenuptial agreements are quite common in the States, Sunny, especially since divorce has become a national pastime and a boon to lawyers who are out to get their cut. In a financial sense, such agreements offer both protection and security.'

They weren't common in Australia. Or perhaps

they were amongst the very wealthy. Not having ever moved in those circles, she simply didn't know.

'If that is your practice here, Bryce, why didn't you offer one to me?' she queried, *the bargain basement bride* tag nagging at her sense of self-worth.

He didn't have a ready reply. Sunny had the disturbing impression that the wheels had just fallen off his train. The silence reeked of a massive recalculation being made. It totally unnerved her. She broke away from him, frightened now of this marriage she had entered into, feeling hopelessly alienated by an attitude of mind she could never be sympathetic to.

She dropped the pretty bridal nosegay onto an armchair. The rings he'd placed on her finger glinted up at her, mocking the 'forever' sentiments she'd given them. Her heart bled for the dream he wasn't giving her and she cursed herself for having been so hasty in choosing this man to be her husband.

'Do you want a financial agreement, Sunny?' he asked in a flat, weary tone. 'I'll see to it right now if it will make you feel more secure.'

Secure! That was such a black joke she might have laughed if it had involved anyone but herself. 'No!' she exploded, wheeling on him as a turbulent rush of emotion demanded he at least understand where *she* was coming from. 'I would be the whore Derek said I was if I let myself be bought like that, and don't you dare treat me like one, Bryce Templar.'

He frowned. His hands lifted in appeal. 'I thought...you seemed upset that I hadn't brought it up with you.'

'If you had, I would never have married you,' she shot back at him in towering contempt. 'It's looking for the out before you're even in. It makes a mockery of the commitment that marriage is supposed to stand for. Especially when children are planned. Especially!' she repeated with passionate conviction.

'That's precisely why I didn't bring it up, Sunny,' he declared, his concern clearing.

'Is it?' she hotly challenged. 'Or am I the windfall that won't cost you as much as Kristen Parrish would have? *The bargain basement bride!*'

He flinched.

For one heart-cramping moment, Sunny thought she had hit the nail right on the head.

Then he exploded into violent rebuttal, his arms slicing the air in scissor-like dismissal. 'I will not have you thinking that of yourself! Nor of me!'

Sunny quivered in shock as he came at her, not having expected to stir such a storm of emotion in him. A calculating man surely stayed in control, but there was nothing at all controlled about his wild gesticulations or the passion pouring from his voice.

'Money didn't once enter into my wanting you. *You,* for yourself, Sunny. I sat there in that conference room yesterday morning, watching you give your presentation, and the whole vibrant warmth of you called to me so strongly...'

'Then?' she squeaked. 'You wanted me then?'

'Yes! So much I was planning to ask you to join me for lunch! Anything to have more of you!'

'But you didn't.'

'No. Because when you stepped off that podium I

saw the engagement ring on your finger. Which meant you belonged to someone else. And I didn't think you were the kind of woman I could *buy* away from a man you were committed to.'

She shook her head, stunned by these revelations.

'You made me hate the thought of marrying Kristen.' His mouth curled around the name in savage disgust. 'Kristen, who kept putting a higher and higher price on having a child in the prenuptial agreement she insisted upon.'

He tore off the silk cravat and unbuttoned his collar as though it were choking him. 'Then…then I was on my way out of the hotel and I saw you confronting some guy at a blackjack table. I saw you take off your ring and hand it back to him.'

'You saw?'

'It stopped me in my tracks. I watched you come towards the lobby and all I could think of was…I *can* have her. I *will* have her.'

She hadn't been mad for thinking what she had in the lobby—Bryce Templar determined on claiming her as his woman.

'If that feels wrong to you, I'm sorry, but it felt very right to me. And I acted on it. What's more…' He hurled off his coat and his fingers attacked the buttons of his vest with speedy efficiency. '…I'll keep acting on it.'

The vest went flying. In an instant he was right in front of her, grasping her upper arms, his eyes blazing with the need to burn away anything standing between them. 'You came with me, Sunny. You wanted me last night. You wanted me this morning. You agreed to marry me. You're my wife.'

It was all true. She stared back at him, overwhelmed by the passion he was emitting. Somehow it didn't matter that there had been ruthless calculation behind everything he'd done, because it was for her...because he wanted her.

'My wife,' he repeated, his voice throbbing with fierce possessiveness. 'And that's how it's going to be.'

He kissed her, and his need poured from his mouth to hers, igniting her own need to have all the worries of this day obliterated, to simply lose herself in the primitive heat of being one with him, as she had been last night, as she could be now...

With a low, animal growl, he scooped her off her feet, carrying her with him, clutching her to his chest, raining kisses on her face and muttering, 'I'll make it right. I'll make it right.'

The frenzied refrain pounded through Sunny's heart, making it swell with a wild kind of joy. She clung to him, kissing him back as feverishly as he kissed her. Nothing had to make sense. This frantic desire had a momentum all its own.

Beside the bed they had shared before, Bryce stood her on her feet to peel off her clothes, and he slowed himself down, taking care, his eyes glittering over her as he removed each garment. 'You are so beautiful to me. Do you know that? Have I told you?'

His hands caressed, sending delicious quivers of anticipation through her. He knew how to touch. He knew how to do everything.

'Yes,' she said. 'Yes. You're beautiful to me, too, Bryce.'

And she did the same to him, stripping off the rest of his clothes, taking the time to glide her hands over his marvellous male body, revelling in his perfect musculature, the gleaming tautness of his skin. She exulted when she felt little tremors running under it, knowing he was as excited by her touch as she was by his. It was especially wonderful to run her fingertips up the impressive strength of his thighs, to hold and stroke and feel the power of his sexuality.

'Sunny...' It was a furred breathing of her name, threaded with barely contained longing. His hands spanned her waist, lifting her up, sliding her body against his. 'Wrap your legs around my hips. I want to feel you hugging me, wanting me...'

She did, with both her arms and her legs, holding his head to the soft cushion of her breasts as he dropped an arm to support her where she was, instinctively balancing both their bodies so he could join them, the insertion so slickly smooth, so incredibly satisfying, so intensely *right*, Sunny closed her eyes and breathed a sigh of utter bliss.

His arms slid up on either side of her spine. 'Lean back. I won't let you fall.'

There was no question of not trusting his strength to hold her wherever he wanted to hold her. She leaned back and his penetration went deeper, increasing the sense of intimate union so exquisitely, Sunny was unaware that angling away from him left her bare breasts tilted perfectly to be reached by his mouth. The heightening of pleasure was enormous when he started kissing them, swinging her body from side to side as he moved from one to the other, creating arcs of intense sensation and building such a rapid escalation of excitement, she was swamped in huge rolling waves of it.

'Oh...oh...oh...' she heard herself gasping, totally beyond doing anything active herself. It felt as though she were absolutely possessed by him, enthralled by the sweet havoc he wrought inside her, and wanting more and more and more of every fantastic sensation he imparted.

He lowered her wildly palpitating body onto the side of the bed, still holding her pinioned to him, and the voluptuous roll of him inside her changed to a fast plummeting rhythm that brought surges of sheer ecstacy, a fierce tumbling of pleasure that engulfed her, and the deep inner beat of him went on and on until suddenly it ebbed into a delicious sea of peace.

She was hopelessly limp when Bryce gathered her to him and moved them both fully onto the bed, turning to lie on his back with Sunny half sprawled on top of him. She could feel his heart thumping under her cheek and it seemed to pulse through her own bloodstream. Into the haze of her mind slid the thought...*This is my husband*...and a sweet contentment accompanied it and lingered.

Sexually, what more could she ask for in a partner? He excited her beyond anything she had ever felt before. And she loved his physique. It was such a pleasure to look at him, feel him, and he was now hers to have and to hold—a fantasy come true—so she had every reason to feel content.

'I think, if you want to save this bridal coronet of flowers, I'd better unpin it,' Bryce gruffly remarked.

'Mmm...'

'It's got a bit bruised, but it did look fantastic on you with the rest of you naked, Sunny. Still like a bride.'

Sexy pleasure in his voice—visual satisfaction as well as physical. Sunny smiled as she felt his fingers move gently through her hair, removing pins. She must have looked like some kind of pagan bride. Which led her to the thought that probably in primitive times, mating for life was all physical. The choice of instinct. Survival.

She certainly would have picked *him* out of any bunch of men. Why should it be any different now? The saleslady at the bridal boutique had it right. She'd won the prize.

Though, in a way, she'd won it because the sleekly glamorous status-holder, Kristen Parrish, had defaulted in the marriage stakes, demanding too big a bride-price. A child-price, as well. Which was particularly offensive to Sunny's way of thinking. In fact, it was a cold, callous calculating thing to say—I won't have your baby unless you pay me big bucks.

If anyone was 'the pig' in this agreement, Sunny decided it was Kristen.

Which raised a niggly little question.

'Bryce?'

'Mmm?' Having removed the coronet of flowers, he was busy gently massaging her scalp where the pins had been.

'Would you have married Kristen if you hadn't met me?'

His chest rose and fell as he deeply inhaled and breathed out a heavy sigh. 'She's gone, Sunny. This is us,' he said emphatically.

She hitched herself up to assure him she wasn't being jealous or going down some negative path. 'I know. And I'm glad it's us. Truly I am.'

'Good!' He looked and sounded relieved.

'I just want to know if you would have gone through with it, lacking me to replace her?'

His face tightened. She saw a flash of grim ruthlessness in his eyes. 'Yes, I would have married her. But given the fortune she was demanding, I would have insisted on getting uncontested custody of any child we had.'

His child. Sunny believed him. In his world, his father's marriages had come and gone, so Bryce probably didn't set much store by them, but a child—*his child*—meant a great deal. And she understood he much preferred a wife who *wanted* to be a mother to his child, simply because being a mother was important to her, having a value beyond money.

His expression softened as he lifted a hand to her face, gently stroking the contours of it. 'I know you'd never hold a child to ransom, Sunny. You want to share. You care what happens. You want what's best. You'd ensure our child has...' He smiled. '...emotional security.'

'Money doesn't give that, Bryce.'

'I know. I want to give our child emotional security, too. Are you willing to throw your pills away now, Sunny?'

Decision time.

It had been a whole day of decisions.

There seemed no point in hesitating over this last one now.

'Yes,' she answered firmly. 'It's what we both got married for, isn't it? To be parents.'

He laughed, his eyes twinkling wickedly. 'Well, there are some fringe benefits, wife of mine.' And he rolled her onto her back, exuding happiness as he began kissing her again. 'I'm going to love every minute of every effort needed for us to make a baby.'

Sunny had no doubt she would revel in the process, too.

'Though the sooner I get you pregnant, the better,' Bryce murmured. 'I want to take that load off my father's mind. And give him a grandchild.'

His father... Bryce's whole motivation for marrying.

A dark concern sliced into Sunny's mind.

What if she didn't get pregnant?

What if she couldn't have children at all?

Everything hung on it.

Everything!

CHAPTER TWELVE

BRYCE was smiling as he picked up the telephone to call his father. *His wife* was still upstairs, getting ready for their flight to Sedona, and he'd left her smiling, too.

No problems left unresolved.

Everything was on track, just as he wanted it.

He dialled the number and Rosita Perez, the resident housekeeper, picked up at the other end.

'Bryce Templar, here. How is my father this morning?'

'A bit poorly, Señor Bryce, but I'd say it's more grumpy humour than anything else. Do you want to speak to him?'

'Yes, I do.'

Bryce waited, happily anticipating improving his father's humour. Good news, it was said, was the best medicine of all.

'About time you called,' came the curt and typical greeting.

Bryce grinned to himself. 'I'm flying to Sedona to have lunch with you. Does that suit?'

'Of course, it suits. Darned carers won't let me get up to anything myself. Doctors meddling all the time. Pack of quacks, if you ask me.'

'I'm bringing my wife with me.'

'Wife? Did you say *wife?*'

'I did. We got married yesterday.'

'Well, now...'

Bryce could hear his father smiling through the mellowed tone. Without a doubt, being presented with what he wanted was a fine lift to his heart.

'...a done deed, eh!' He actually chuckled. 'Smart move, talking Kristen out of the big showcase wedding she was planning. Lot of nonsense.'

'I didn't marry Kristen.'

'What?'

'I said...*I didn't marry Kristen.* I broke off my engagement to her and married a much better choice for me—Sunny York.'

'What? Who?' His voice rose several decibels.

'Calm down, Dad. You wanted me married. I'm married. To a woman who not only has beauty and brains, but also a warm heart. Even her name is warm—Sunny. Please remember it when we visit.'

'Sunny who?'

'Sunny York. Now Sunny Templar.'

'I don't know any Yorks.' His tone had dropped to querulous.

'You'll get to know her if you treat her nicely.'

'Where'd you meet her?'

'Here in Las Vegas.'

'She's not a showgirl, is she?' Dark suspicion winging in.

'No. Sunny actually works for our company. From the Sydney branch. An Australian.'

'That's going a bit far afield, isn't it? What's wrong with a good American woman?'

'There's nothing wrong with a good American

woman. It just so happens that this Australian woman has more appeal to me than any other female inhabitant of this planet.'

'This sounds too impetuous.' A muttered grumble. 'Good stock, the Parrishes. What do you know about this York family? Do they breed well?'

'Sunny has two sisters with children. Satisfied?'

'Better to have tests done.'

'Did you get *my* mother to have a fertility test?'

'Different times then. You said so yourself. Besides, I was younger than you. How old is this wife of yours?'

'Plenty young enough to have children. And so am I.'

'Huh! Grey in your hair already. Better get started.'

'We intend to.'

'Good!'

'I'm glad you approve,' Bryce said very dryly.

'Don't come that tone with me, boy. You needed pushing into doing the right thing. You just bring this wife along to me and I'll see if you've done it.'

'Her name is Sunny, Dad. You'd better get it right, too, or we won't be staying long.'

'Are you threatening me?'

'No. Just telling you how it is.'

'I hope you're not being led around by the brain below your belt, Bryce.'

'Oh, I think both brains are in fine operation.'

His father snorted. 'When can I expect you?'

'Around noon.'

'I'll be looking forward to it.'

'That was the idea.'

He heard his father chuckling as he put the receiver down.

It gave Bryce's heart a lift.

It *was* good that he'd got married. All the better that he was married to Sunny—a wife worth having in every sense. Producing a grandchild for his father would be no hardship. The trick was to get Sunny pregnant immediately. He'd wasted three months on Kristen. His father was counting his life in terms of one year, which meant there were only nine months left.

Bryce decided he could afford to take a week off work for a honeymoon. Making a baby with Sunny was more important than anything else.

Sunny was all packed and ready to leave for Sedona. Meeting and having lunch with Bryce's father—Will Templar himself—was scary enough without getting her nerves into more of a twist. She didn't have to check her laptop computer for e-mail. It was probably better not to.

Back home in Sydney it was still the middle of the night, so if there was some response from her family about her marriage to Bryce, they wouldn't be looking for any reply from her for many hours yet. Although she'd sent the announcement and the scanned wedding photograph over twelve hours ago, there was no guarantee that her sister, Alyssa, or her husband, John, had even turned on their home computer since then.

Better not to look.

She checked the bathroom once more in case she'd

left something behind. She re-checked her appearance, hoping Will Templar would not find any fault in his new daughter-in-law. Her hair hadn't moved too much out of yesterday's styling for the wedding. Her make-up looked good, if anything understated, but that would probably meet more approval than overstated.

She was wearing one of her conference suits—not the yellow one which she considered too business-like for such a personal meeting. This was a pantsuit in a terracotta gaberdine mixture that didn't crush. Smart casual. The cream silk blouse with its geometric print in green and gold and terracotta gave it a classy touch. She hoped she looked right as Bryce's wife.

Bryce Templar's wife...

Her mind flitted to the e-mail she had sent to her family—short and to the point.

'Today I married Bryce Templar, CEO of Templar Resources. See attached wedding photograph. Will explain everything when I see you. Bryce simply swept me off my feet. As soon as we can he'll be flying home with me to meet the family and help me settle everything there. We'll see you then.'

She walked back into the bedroom and stared at the laptop computer again. What could they say, anyway? A whole pile of recriminations wasn't going to change anything. It was a done deed. Maybe they'd congratulate her.

The laptop stared back—Pandora's box.

Sunny took a deep breath. Not looking was really cowardly. Besides, her nerves couldn't get into much more of a twist. She acted fast, slinging the laptop onto the dressing-table, plugging it in, opening up, switching on, her fingers moving like lightning over the keyboard. The dialling tone seemed to mock her impatience, playing its infuriating little ditty.

Checking incoming messages.

One clicking across the screen.

From Alyssa!

Sunny's heart skipped all over the place as her eyes skated over the words.

Wow! Some bombshell! I called Mum and she cried over missing the wedding but she says to tell you if you're happy she's happy for you and she'll look forward to meeting your new husband.

I called Nadine and she thinks you're crazy for rushing into it. You should have brought him home first. But she wishes you all the best and hopes you haven't made a *big* mistake.

I took one look at the wedding photograph and thought, If I didn't have John—that guy you've married could sweep me off my feet any day. Or night. And that sure is some ring on your finger! Good for you, Sunny.

Lots of love and I can't wait to see him in the flesh!

Sunny breathed a sigh of huge relief. It was okay. They accepted it. And after a while her mother may well be relieved not to have had the expense of another wedding. Paying for her sisters' weddings had been a struggle financially. Sunny had helped out as much as her mother would let her.

She smiled down at the fabulous emerald ring on her finger. It was certainly a statement that none of her family would miss, with its obvious message that Sunny had done very well for herself with the CEO of Templar Resources. Not that money was any yardstick for a successful marriage. It bought things but it couldn't buy happiness.

As for Nadine's hope that she hadn't made a big mistake, well, Sunny hoped that, too, but she wasn't going to let her mind drift down that negative path. She and Bryce had a lot of positive things going for them and they both wanted the marriage to work, especially with becoming parents. Rather than hoping she hadn't made a big mistake, Sunny hoped she'd made the best decision she'd ever made in her life.

She quickly typed a reply—'Thanks, Alyssa. I'll be in touch with details before Bryce and I fly home. 'Bye for now. Love, Sunny.'

Having sent it off, she packed up the laptop again and was just setting it down with the rest of her luggage when she heard Bryce coming up the stairs. She swung to face him as he came through the doorway and was instantly hit anew by his strong sexual impact. Dressed in fawn slacks and a clingy green sports shirt, his magnificent physique seemed to leap out at her, and the grin on his handsome face gave it a magnetic attraction.

Alyssa's words zipped through her mind—*he could sweep me off my feet any day. Or night.*

He'd done just that, Sunny thought, and she didn't

regret a second of it. In fact, if he wanted to do it right now...

'I've called for a bellboy. Are you all packed, ready to leave?'

Her hands fluttered, appealing for his opinion. 'Do I look right to meet your father?'

His eyes simmered over her, causing her breasts to peak into hard nubs and sending tremulous little ripples down her thighs.

'Perfect!' he declared huskily, his gaze finally lifting to sear away any doubts or fears in hers. 'Don't worry about what my father thinks, Sunny. You're *the wife* I want. He'll see that fast enough.'

He walked towards her, emanating a ruthless determination that she was coming to recognise. Nothing was going to shake Bryce from what *he* wanted. Her heart quivered with the knowledge that he'd wanted her from the moment she'd come to his notice, and now she was his.

But would she stay his if she couldn't give him the child he wanted?

No negative thoughts, she savagely berated herself as he drew her into his embrace, the green eyes warmly smiling at her, promising there was no possible conflict of interests in this meeting with his father.

'He's looking forward to our visit.'

'Yes...well...it will be interesting.' She managed a teasing little smile in response. 'Father and son.'

Bryce laughed. 'Always a testing ground.' He raised quizzing brows. 'Any reply from your family?'

'Shock/surprise, but best wishes and looking forward to meeting you.'

'So…no problems there.' His eyes glittered satisfaction. 'I've booked us into the L'Auberge Inn at Sedona for tonight.'

This was startling news. 'We're not staying with your father?'

'What? On our honeymoon?'

'We're having a honeymoon?'

'After the wedding comes a honeymoon,' Bryce asserted. 'We are going to do everything right, Sunny.'

And as he bent to kiss her, Sunny was thinking, surely nothing could go wrong when Bryce was so intent on making everything right.

CHAPTER THIRTEEN

THE fantastic red rock formations around Sedona just seemed to suddenly rise out of the Arizona desert, as startling and as stunning as The Olgas rising out of the desert in the red centre of Australia. Sunny was amazed by what was wrought by time and nature, and the likeness to parts of the Outback.

She had a marvellous view of it all from the plane before it set down at the airport, which was surprisingly situated on top of a hill overlooking the township. They were met by Will Templar's chauffeur who loaded both them and their luggage into a very plush Cadillac. It was a very scenic drive, down the hill, through the town which seemed to be spread around a T-junction, then up another hill and finally into the driveway of a huge sprawling house built of stone and wood.

It commanded a spectacular view in every direction, and there were big windows and furnished porches to take advantage of it from both inside and out of doors. A large swimming pool occupied one side of the grounds with what looked like sophisticated barbecue facilities under a roofed area nearby. Everything projected a casual lifestyle, not a formal one, which set Sunny more at ease.

They were met at the front door by a middle-aged

Mexican woman whom Bryce introduced as Rosita Perez, adding that Rosita ran the household.

She beamed at Sunny. 'You are very welcome. *Very* welcome. Such wonderful news!' Her dark eyes twinkled at Bryce. 'Señor Will wants fajitas for lunch. It is a good sign.'

Sunny smiled and nodded. She didn't know about fajitas but the warmth of the greeting helped to calm the butterflies in her stomach.

'Where is he?' Bryce asked.

'On his favourite balcony. I have set out drinks and dips there. Go on....' Rosita shooed them forward. '...he is waiting.'

They walked through a huge living room; big stone fireplace, big furniture in wood and black leather, brightly patterned scatter cushions and rugs featuring Indian motifs.

'What are fajitas?' Sunny whispered.

Bryce grinned. 'Dad's favourite dish. Spicy meat and vegetables wrapped in a kind of tortilla.'

'How spicy?'

'Not too spicy.' His eyes teased her concern. 'There'll be other dishes for you to choose from, so don't worry. You'll get fed.'

'Being nervous makes me hungry.'

'The avocado dip Rosita makes is great. So is the corn one. Get stuck into them,' he advised, his eyes positively laughing as he opened one of the glass doors to the designated balcony.

Sunny took a deep breath and stepped out.

It was a very wide, spacious balcony, holding a dark green wrought-iron-and-glass dining table, with six matching chairs cushioned in green and white. There were occasional tables, as well, serving groups of sun loungers upholstered in the same colours. However, the drinks and food Rosita had mentioned were set out on the dining table.

The rustle of a newspaper being put down was the first indication of Will Templar's presence. She swung her gaze towards the sound and caught the movement of legs being swung off one of the loungers...long legs encased in light grey trousers. Behind her the door closed and she sensed Bryce stepping to her side as the man on the lounger rose to his feet.

Her first thought was, this will be Bryce thirty years from now. The likeness between father and son was striking, despite the older man's white hair and the illness that had stripped him of extra weight that would have normally filled out his face and powerful frame.

They shared the same impressive height and strong facial features, as well as the air of being in command of their world. Will Templar's heart condition certainly hadn't diminished that, Sunny thought, and fancied these father and son meetings could sometimes develop into the clash of the Titans.

'Sunny, this is my father,' Bryce said casually. 'Dad, this is my wife.'

In the face of such an intimidating authority figure, all her sales training leapt to the fore, pushing her into taking the initiative. 'Hi,' she said warmly, smiling as she moved forward to offer her hand and focusing directly on his eyes, which to her surprise were a silvery grey, different to Bryce's. 'I've been looking forward to meeting you, Mr. Templar.'

He took her hand and held it, seemingly amused by her brashly open approach. 'Impressive. A sunny disposition...' His gaze flicked to Bryce, one brow lifting. '...and the legs of a showgirl.'

'Ignore that, Sunny,' Bryce returned dryly. 'My father has a fixation on showgirls.'

Will Templar laughed and pressed her hand reassuringly. 'My son made the claim of beauty and brains. Since both are in evidence, I just thought I'd add my observations to the list. A very great pleasure to meet you, Sunny.'

The feeling of being patronised instantly raised Sunny's hackles. 'Is this a case of let the fun begin between you two?' she challenged. 'Shall I just sit down and eat while you get on with it?'

'Sassy, too.' Will Templar grinned, patting her hand in approval. 'I think I'll let you entertain me instead.'

'If you're not careful, Dad, Sunny may very well eat you for lunch.'

'I did notice her teeth, my boy,' he retorted good-humouredly. 'A smile to dazzle you with before chomping.'

'Beware the bite,' Bryce tossed back at him. 'Mine, too.'

'I do love a good fight,' Will Templar confided to Sunny, wrapping her arm around his as he drew her towards the table. 'Especially when I win.'

'I'm the winner here,' Bryce declared, his eyes hotly assuring Sunny she was the top prize to him.

'I can see that,' his father conceded. 'But who spurred you on to take a wife?'

Again the feeling of being a mere cipher between them goaded Sunny into further speech. 'Actually, Mr. Templar, I took Bryce as my husband.'

'What?' He looked flabbergasted at her temerity.

Sunny smiled. 'You could call it a mutual taking. I did have equal say in it, you know.'

Bryce laughed.

His father looked askance at her. 'You have a very smart tongue.'

'Smart brain, too,' Bryce chimed in. 'What would you like to drink, Dad?'

'I've got to stick to juice.'

'Sunny?'

'I'll have juice, too, thanks, Bryce.'

'I had Rosita bring out a bottle of Krug champagne,' his father pointed out.

'Lovely,' Sunny warmly approved, 'but not on an empty stomach.'

He pulled out a chair from the table and waved her to it. 'Then sit down and eat,' he commanded, put out at not having everything go his way.

Sunny grinned at him. 'Thank you.'

He shook a finger at her. 'You...are a very provocative young woman.'

'You mean...not a yes-woman?' Sunny tilted at him before reaching for a corn chip and the avocado dip. 'Having a mind of my own has always worked better for me, Mr. Templar. I see no reason to give it up just because I married your son.'

She coated the chip with dip and popped it in her

mouth, feeling highly invigorated for having stood up for herself.

'Here's your juice, Sunny.' Bryce set a filled glass in front of her.

'What about mine?' his father growled. 'I'm the invalid around here.'

'I thought you were fighting fit, Dad.'

'Two against one is not a fair fight.'

'You asked for it. Now if you'll stop assuming Sunny is a walkover, we could have a really pleasant lunch together.'

'Just testing her out.' He settled himself on the chair at the head of the table, gesticulating at Bryce. 'You bring a stranger into the family. How am I supposed to know her mettle if I don't test her out?'

'You could try trusting my judgment,' came the ready advice as Bryce set a glass of juice in front of his father.

'Huh! Men can get blinded by a woman's beauty.'

Bryce raised an eyebrow at Sunny. 'Am I blind?'

She grinned at him, having just tried the corn dip and found it as delicious as the avocado one. 'No. Just besotted. But that's okay because I'm besotted, too.'

Will Templar barked with laughter, vastly amused by the exchange. 'Oh, that's good! Very good! If you're not careful, Bryce, she'll be giving you the rounds of the kitchen.'

'A novel thought,' he retorted, pulling out the chair at the foot of the table and relaxing onto it.

'Novelty wears off,' came the sardonic reply. 'She might be compliant now, but...'

'You know, Mr. Templar,' Sunny cut in sweetly. 'Where I come from, it's rude to talk over a person as though she's not there.'

His silvery grey eyes narrowed on her. 'No respect for authority. I've heard that about Australians.'

'Then you've heard wrong. We do respect an authority who shows us respect.'

'Just what position do you hold in our company, young woman?'

'I do sales presentations. And I work hard at commanding respect, Mr. Templar. I do not lie down and let people steamroll over me.'

'But you're married to Bryce now,' he said sharply. 'Do you expect to keep on working?'

'Do you have a problem with that, Mr. Templar?'

'What about children? Do you figure on having any?'

She flashed a look at Bryce who smiled back at her, confident of her reply and perfectly content to let the conversation run without his interference. His eyes said she was doing fine with his father.

'Yes, we do,' she said, smiling her own pleasure in the prospect of having a family with Bryce.

'Do you intend on working then?'

'Being a mother will have priority, but it does take nine months to make a baby, Mr. Templar. Do you think I should twiddle my thumbs until one arrives?'

He frowned. 'Got to take care of yourself during pregnancy,' he said bruskly. 'My first wife—Bryce's mother—had a hard time of it. Kidney problems. Shouldn't have had a child at all. Died when Bryce was only a toddler.'

The brusk tone carried shades of old pain, instantly cooling Sunny's fighting instincts and stirring her sympathy. 'I'm sorry,' she said softly. 'I really want to have a baby, so you can be sure I'll take every care when I do fall pregnant, Mr. Templar.'

'Yes, well, no time to waste,' he said gruffly. 'Bryce isn't getting any younger. He's thirty-four, you know. Should have started a family years ago.'

'A bit difficult when I only met Sunny this week,' Bryce drawled, his eyes mocking his father's contention. 'And you can hardly accuse me of wasting time once I met the right woman.'

His gaze shifted to Sunny and she basked in the warmth of it, feeling more and more that she truly was right for him, and he was right for her. A hasty marriage it might be, but she certainly didn't repent her decision...yet.

'Got an answer for everything,' Will Templar grumbled. 'Sunny, you're hogging those dips. While I'm happy to see you have a healthy appetite, I like them, too.'

'Would you like me to spread some on the chips for you?' Sunny immediately offered.

'I can help myself if you'll kindly pass them up.'

'Not thinking of yourself as an invalid anymore?' Bryce archly commented as Sunny obliged.

'I can handle a bit of finger food.' He glowered at Bryce. 'I see you're feeling on top of things, just because you got married.'

'I generally am on top of things, Dad. I work at it. Which is why you made me CEO, remember?'

'Well, don't be getting too cocky about

it…counting chickens before they hatch. Damian called me yesterday.'

'Nice for you that he keeps in touch.' Bryce slanted a wry smile at Sunny. 'Damian is my half-brother. Dad's son by his third wife.'

'A very caring son, too,' Will Templar declared, pausing to give the statement weight, and eyeing Bryce with a very definite glint of challenge. 'Told me his wife's pregnant.'

Bryce nodded affably. 'I must call and congratulate them.'

'Giving me a grandchild before you do.'

Sunny sensed the threat behind the words and instantly felt uneasy. Was Will Templar playing one son off against another, with the position of CEO as the prize? If so, there was a factor in his marriage decision that Bryce hadn't told her about. She looked sharply at him but discerned no rise of tension in his demeanour.

He smiled, maintaining an affable front. 'I'm glad you'll be getting in some practice as a grandfather before Sunny and I have a child. In fact, maybe we should wait a while, simply enjoy having each other before Sunny gets pregnant. I believe a baby needs to be welcomed and loved for itself…' His lips were still curved into a smile but his eyes hardened to green flint as he softly added, '…not used as a pawn.'

Suddenly the air between father and son was so thick with threat and counter-threat, it could have been cut with a knife.

Sunny knew intuitively Bryce would not back off. And she didn't want him to. What he'd stated was what she believed, as well, although she didn't really want to wait. Not long, anyway. All the same, she understood that pleasing his father was one thing, being dictated to was quite another. Bryce would not be the man he was if he tamely succumbed to his father's string-pulling.

She was startled when Will Templar abruptly switched his focus to her. 'Do you want to wait a while, Sunny?' he demanded rather than asked.

'I think husband and wife should be in total agreement on when they have a baby and it's no one else's business but theirs,' she said slowly, keeping her wits alert to the undercurrents. 'I'm sure Bryce would consider what I want, every bit as much as I would consider what he wants.'

Will Templar leaned forward, boring in. 'Do you realise I still have the power to strip Bryce of his position in the company?'

Sunny felt her spine bristling. Her eyes locked onto the older man's and fought fire with fire. 'I didn't marry Bryce for *his position,* Mr. Templar.'

'What did you marry him for?'

'I fancied him rotten and I thought he'd make a great father for the children I want.'

'You fancied him *rotten?*'

Either he was unfamiliar with the term or she'd knocked him off his power perch. Sunny decided to play her hand to the hilt.

'Mmm…' She gave Bryce a smouldering look. 'He has a way of inspiring the most terrible lust in me.'

He smouldered right back. 'The inspiration goes both ways.'

'Enough!' Will Templar snapped. 'You don't have to prove you're *besotted* with each other at my table!'

Bryce shrugged. 'Actually, we don't have to prove anything, Dad. We just came to visit.'

'Fine visit this is...not even opening the bottle of champagne.'

'I'll be happy to open it,' Bryce said, lifting the bottle out of the ice bucket. 'Ready for a glass now, Sunny?'

'Yes. Thank you. These dips really are delicious.'

'Are you always so direct?' his father demanded of her.

Sunny frowned quizzically at him. 'Weren't you being direct with me, Mr. Templar?'

He looked somewhat disgruntled. 'Just testing your mettle.'

'Did I pass the test?'

He snorted. 'It's plain you and Bryce are two of a kind.'

'Is that good or bad?' Sunny queried.

For the first time she saw a flash of respect in his eyes. 'You can call me Will.'

'Thank you.' She smiled warmly. 'I take that as a real compliment.'

'So you should.' He visibly thawed. 'Just see that boy of mine starts fathering real soon. Can't wait forever for a grandchild, you know.'

From which Sunny deduced it was Bryce's child he most wanted to see, not Damian's.

That thought stayed with her long after the lunch visit was over and Will Templar had conveyed his rather crotchety blessing on the marriage and expressed his pointed hope that their honeymoon would be *productive*.

The chauffeur transported them to the L'Auberge Inn which was nestled along the bank of a pretty, tree-lined creek and surrounded by towering red cliffs. It had a European-style lodge, supplying luxurious amenities for resident guests, and the secluded cottage Bryce had booked for the night was very romantically furnished in a rich, French provincial style.

'May I say how delighted I am that you fancy me rotten,' Bryce tossed at her the moment they were alone.

She laughed and repeated her smouldering look. 'Your father clearly does not see you through the eyes of a woman.'

'I'm only interested in your eyes, Sunny,' he said seriously, enfolding her in his embrace. 'You handled my father brilliantly, but...can I believe every word you said?'

'You know the wanting is real, Bryce. How could it not be when...' She blushed at the memories of her deeply primitive response to him.

He reached up and ran his fingertips over the self-conscious heat, his eyes burning into hers as he softly asked, 'Did you fancy me rotten before you broke with Derek?'

Her skin became even hotter under his questing touch. The intensity he was projecting seeded a wild thought. Was he jealous of the relationship she'd had with her ex-fiancé?

'You must be aware of how attractive you are physically, Bryce. I think any woman would fancy you. The saleslady who sold me my wedding dress certainly did. But I didn't know you in any personal sense...'

'And now that you do?'

'Derek belongs in the past. It's you I want.'

She wound her arms around his neck and kissed him to prove there was no looking back on her part. He was her husband now and she wanted no other.

Bryce stormed her mouth with a passionate possessiveness that swiftly moved into much more than a kiss. They made love in a frenzy of desire for each other, craving an affirmation that their marriage was right and always would be.

It was hours later, when they were dressing for dinner—Bryce insisting she wear the cream lace gown again for the six-course 'wedding feast' he planned to order at the gourmet restaurant in the lodge—that Sunny recalled the question raised at lunch with Will Templar.

'Are you in competition with your half-brother, Bryce?' she asked bluntly, wanting to know the truth.

'Damian?' He looked amused, his eyes mocking the suggestion as he answered, 'My father cares too much for Templar Resources to ever put Damian in control of it, Sunny. He knows it. I know it. It's not an option.'

'Then why did he threaten it?'

Bryce shrugged. 'It's simply a measure of how much he wants me to have a child.'

She frowned. 'You played it like a power game, saying we might wait.'

'A gift is one thing, a pressured demand quite another.'

'What would you do if he did give the CEO position to Damian?'

'Go into opposition. In effect, my father would lose me.'

And you would lose him, she thought.

'He won't go that far, Sunny. Don't worry about it.'

All the same, she couldn't help thinking it would be best—easier all around—if they did have a child straight away. And Bryce had to be thinking that, too.

A productive honeymoon…

CHAPTER FOURTEEN

SUNNY was not the least bit nervous about introducing Bryce to her family. She was happily looking forward to it as she settled herself to sleep away some of the hours on the long flight from Los Angeles to Sydney. Travelling first class gave her much more leg room to make herself comfortable and the wider seat took away the sense of feeling cramped. She tucked the airline blanket around her, sighed contentedly and closed her eyes.

'Sweet dreams,' Bryce murmured indulgently, leaning over from the seat beside her to drop a kiss on her forehead.

She smiled. He made her feel loved. During their whole honeymoon, which Bryce had extended to ten days, he had made her feel loved, and she knew now that she loved him. The words had not been spoken but that didn't matter. The feeling was there, which meant nothing was missing from their marriage...except a baby...and since she may well have conceived already, Sunny was not going to let that concern weigh on her mind.

She had such good memories to dwell on; action-packed days, touring the rim of the awesome Grand Canyon, cruising Lake Powell, hiking the trails through the breathtaking beauty of the hoodoos at Bryce Canyon—well named, her husband had jokingly declared—and absolutely blissful nights, revelling in the sensual pleasures of intimacy.

Her sleep on the plane was deep and untroubled. She awoke with a sense of well-being that stayed with her until the plane circled over Sydney before landing. The view of the harbour, the great Coat-hanger bridge, the gleaming white sails of the opera house, the sparkling blue of the water...it suddenly grabbed her heart and gave it a twist. *This was home.* What had she done, abandoning it for a host of unknowns?

A rush of strong emotion brought tears to her eyes. She blinked rapidly to drive them back. It was silly to let a familiar view get to her like this. People were more important than places. She had Bryce. And right on that thought, he reached across, took her hand, and gently squeezed it.

'A touch homesick?'

'It's just so beautiful,' she excused.

'Yes, it is. One of the most beautiful cities in the world,' he said warmly. 'We will be back, many times, Sunny.'

She flashed him a watery smile. 'It's okay. I do want to be with you, Bryce.'

He nodded and interlaced his fingers with hers, reinforcing their togetherness. There were times when he seemed ruthlessly intent on not allowing anything to shadow it.

He had arbitrarily dismissed the idea of staying in her Sydney apartment, booking an executive suite at the Regent Hotel for the duration of their visit. Sunny suspected he didn't care to be anywhere Derek had been, but he argued comfort and the fact that it would complicate her task of clearing everything out and ending the lease. Which was true enough.

She was thankful she and Derek had maintained separate apartments, never actually living together. At least she didn't have the complication of dividing up possessions. That would have been really messy. They had never swapped door keys, either, which was probably just as well, given their bitter parting. Sunny saw no problems in doing what had to be done today.

Although they had left Los Angeles on Wednesday night, crossing the dateline meant they were arriving in Sydney on Friday morning, and they'd be flying out again on Sunday. A packing company had already been lined up to help her at the apartment. Bryce wanted to spend the day in the Sydney headquarters of Templar Resources and he offered to collect her personal belongings from the office where she had worked.

This, Sunny realised, neatly avoided any unpleasant encounter between her and Derek, so she had agreed to the plan, but she did regret missing the opportunity to say goodbye to the people she had been friendly with. Though they were mostly men who would probably side with Derek, she argued to herself. Since her life was now with Bryce, it seemed wiser to simply stay out of the situation.

The plane landed safely at Mascot Airport. A limousine took them to the Regent Hotel. They had time to freshen up, eat a light second breakfast, and go over their plans for the day in case something had not been thought of. Satisfied that everything was in hand, Bryce left for head office and Sunny took a taxi to her old neighbourhood in the suburb of Drummoyne, only a short trip from the centre of the city.

It was strange, moving around the apartment she had occupied for the past four years, wondering what to do with everything she had collected here. There was no point in taking anything but clothes, photo albums and those personal possessions which were especially dear to her. Having spent the last day before their flight to Sydney at Bryce's home in Santa Monica, Sunny was only too aware that it wanted for nothing.

Bryce had advised sending her surplus stuff to a charity but she didn't feel right about that now. It was like irrevocably sweeping out her past—everything that had made up her life before she had gone to Las Vegas. It seemed like saying none of it had any value anymore—all she'd worked for over many years. To just get rid of it because Bryce could provide more and better…it simply didn't sit well with her.

While she waited for the packing people to arrive, she telephoned her mother, letting her know what was happening and asking if there was anything she would like from the apartment. To Sunny's intense relief, her mother suggested sending everything to her. It could be stored in the garage and the whole family could pick and choose what they could use.

'Better we keep it for you,' her mother added. 'You never know, dear. You might not be happy living so far away in another country.'

'Mum, I'm married,' Sunny protested.

'Yes, and I'm sure you're wildly in love. I truly hope this marriage works out wonderfully for you,

Sunny, but...it was rather hasty, dear. And he is an American, not...well, not what you're used to. If sometime in the future you want to come back home...'

'I'm not thinking like that, Mum.'

'I understand, dear. I'd just feel better about it if we keep things for you.'

Insurance against some unforeseen future?

Sunny frowned. Did she herself feel that? The idea warred with her sense of commitment, yet...who could really know what the future held? All she knew was that keeping her things did make her feel more comfortable.

'Okay, Mum. The boxes should arrive this afternoon.' Her mother and sisters lived at Quakers Hill, on the western outskirts of Sydney, not more than an hour away if the truck went there directly. 'Will you be home to direct where they're to be stored?'

'Yes, I'll be home. What time can I expect you and Bryce tomorrow?'

'What time do you want us there?'

'In time for morning tea. Say ten-thirty? I'm cooking your favourite carrot cake this afternoon.'

'Thanks, Mum. That's great! We'll be there soon after ten.'

'If you've got the time, Sunny, call your sisters, too. They're dying to chat to you.'

'I'll try. 'Bye for now.'

With the storage decision made, Sunny threw herself into sorting out what clothes she should take with her now, and what was to be boxed up and sent to her. As arranged, two men from the packing company turned up at ten o'clock and were amazingly efficient at their job; wrapping breakables, grouping things for easy labelling, even boxing the furniture in thick cardboard so nothing could be damaged.

By one o'clock the apartment was completely cleared. The men even carried the suitcases she'd packed down to her car for her. She drove to the local shopping centre, had a quick lunch, then dropped into the real estate agency which handled the lease of her apartment. After handing in her keys there, arranging for cleaning and settling what was owing, Sunny only had one item left on her business agenda—returning the company car which had been part of her salary package.

It was easy, at this point, to simply follow Bryce's advice. She returned to the hotel, had her luggage sent up to the suite, and instructed the concierge that the car was to be picked up by the Templar Resources company. Having now completely dismantled her previous life in Sydney, Sunny suddenly felt drained. Jetlag, she told herself, and retired to their suite to sleep it off.

Except sleep eluded her and she remembered she hadn't yet called her sisters. Or any of her old girl-friends! She started with Alyssa who wanted to hear all about her honeymoon and bubbled on about how marvellous it must be to have a really wealthy husband who could just do what he wanted without counting the cost.

'Bryce does work, too, you know,' Sunny said dryly. 'A CEO doesn't have a lot of leisure time. This was our honeymoon, Alyssa.'

'Yes, but let's face it, Sunny. Derek couldn't have given you all that. And talking of work, did you know he'd resigned from Templar Resources?'

Sunny frowned over that piece of information. 'How could I know when I've been out of the country? And how do you know, Alyssa?'

'Nadine found out. She felt sorry for him and called him.'

'I wish she hadn't done that.'

'Well, you were engaged to him for months, Sunny. Your whirlwind marriage to Bryce was a bit of a shock.'

'Derek spent every spare minute in Las Vegas gambling. Plus time he should have spent at the conference, too. Did he tell Nadine that?' Sunny demanded sharply, annoyed that her youngest sister had gone behind her back to Derek, instead of waiting for her to come home.

'Hey! I didn't do it,' Alyssa protested. 'I just thought you might want to know Derek had left your husband's company. Pride, I guess.'

A niggle of concern made Sunny ask, 'Has he got a job somewhere else?'

'He said he was going to work for the opposition. Beat Templar Resources at their own game. He was angry. You can't exactly blame him.'

Yes, I can, Sunny thought, remembering how he had ignored and neglected her in favour of roulette and blackjack and whatever other games he'd played.

'After what he did in Vegas, resigning was probably the best move he could make. He was well on the way to inviting being sacked, in my opinion,' she remarked stonily.

'That bad, huh?'

'Yes. I just hope he can stay out of casinos and get his life together again.'

'You still care for him?'

'No. Derek killed off any caring when...' She stopped, shying away from the ugly memory of the confrontation in the MGM lobby. She took a deep breath before firmly stating, 'I really don't want to talk about Derek, Alyssa. That's over.'

'Okay. That's fine with me,' came the quick reply. 'I'm really looking forward to meeting Bryce tomorrow.'

'Good. We'll be at Mum's about ten. See you then, Alyssa.'

Still vexed over Nadine's action, Sunny had no inclination whatsoever to call her other sister. Nadine could wait for tomorrow for whatever fuel she wanted for more gossip. She spent a couple of happy hours telephoning her long-time girlfriends, telling them her news, giving them her new address in Santa Monica and promising to keep in touch. The contact lifted her spirits. She wasn't cut off from her old life. It was simply a matter of making adjustments.

Bryce came back from the office in good spirits, too, pleased with the meeting he'd had with the managing director, and the business being done in this branch of Templar Resources. They had an early dinner and talked over what position Sunny could take on in the Los Angeles office, discussing various exciting options.

All in all, Sunny went to bed that night a happy woman, and her happiness with her new husband was shiningly evident at the family gathering the next day. Bryce's personal charisma was so powerful, doubts about *her* hasty marriage were obviously squashed within minutes, wariness switching almost instantly to pleasure in his company. Even her brothers-in-law were impressed, keen to ask Bryce's opinion on anything and everything.

He was especially good with her sisters' children, paying kind attention to the toddlers when they demanded it. Sunny was highly gratified that he fitted in as one of the family, though she doubted Bryce was used to sitting in an ordinary middle-class home, nor having the kind of rowdy lunch her family engaged in.

'Well, he's certainly something,' her mother acknowledged, when the four women were in the kitchen cleaning up after a very elaborate and celebratory meal. Her eyes twinkled delighted approval as she gave Sunny a hug.

'A hunk plus!' Alyssa agreed, rolling her eyes appreciatively.

'Yes, I can see why Derek got his nose out of joint when Bryce stopped him from seeing you,' Nadine dryly commented.

Sunny gave her an exasperated look. 'Bryce didn't *stop* Derek from seeing me. Derek waylaid us and did his nasty best to turn Bryce against me. Which, I'm thankful to say he failed to do.'

Nadine grimaced. 'I meant the night before when Derek followed your luggage to the MGM Hotel. He wanted to make up with you, and Bryce blocked him out.'

Sunny's mind whirled, remembering Bryce had left her in the bath, saying he'd been called down to the lobby to deal with an urgent problem. Derek... demanding to see her? Wanting to right the wrongs between them?

What had Bryce said to him?

Was this why Derek had been so virulent the next morning? So virulent, she had agreed to marry Bryce then and there!

'To be faced with Bryce...' Nadine went on with a shrug. '...poor Derek simply wasn't a match for him.'

'No, he's not,' Sunny grated. 'And I wish you'd drop the subject of *poor* Derek, Nadine. I was running a very *poor* second to his gambling addiction before I even met Bryce.'

'Sorry. I just meant...well, I'd choose Bryce, too.' She grinned to smooth over her gaffe. 'Who wouldn't?'

It was a question Sunny kept asking all afternoon—*who wouldn't?*—but the sparkle had gone out of the day for her. Bryce hadn't exactly lied about Derek's first foray to the MGM Hotel, but he had certainly omitted telling her. She might not have chosen to see Derek that night, but Bryce had clearly removed any choice, ruthlessly removed it, intent on keeping her with him until...until she married him.

Why?

Not out of love for her.

He needed a wife to please his father.

Kristen was demanding too much.

He preferred Sunny...*the bargain basement bride!*

It was difficult to keep up a facade of happily wedded bliss while this inner torment churned through
her, but Sunny managed it. Pride made her keep pretending everything was perfect, though she barely
kept her own tears at bay when her mother got teary
at their leave-taking. It was an enormous relief when
the chauffeured limousine pulled away from her
cheerfully waving family and she could relax back in
the plushly cushioned seat and close her eyes.

'Exhausted?' Bryce asked sympathetically.

'Yes,' she muttered, keeping her eyes shut, not
wanting to look at him.

As he had in the plane, he took her hand, interlac-
ing their fingers in a possessive grip. Sunny raised her
lashes a little to stare down at the linked hands, at the
emerald ring glinting up at her. She was married to
this man, committed to having a family with him. If
she didn't have his love, at the very least she needed
honesty from him.

'I thought the day went well,' he commented.

'Yes, you handled my family brilliantly.'

It was what he'd said of her meeting with his father. He'd probably handled *her* brilliantly, too, all
along, from the moment he decided she should be his
wife instead of Kristen.

'It wasn't hard. They're nice people.'

'I'm glad you think so.'

'Need some quiet time now?'

'Yes.'

He said nothing more until they walked into their

hotel suite and the door was closed behind them. Sunny was working herself up to confront him with what Nadine had told her when he softly asked, 'Want to tell me what's wrong?'

The question hit all the raw places in Sunny's heart. She swung on him, words shooting out of her mouth in a bitter spurt. 'What? So you can fix it, Bryce?' Her eyes hotly accused as her tongue ran on. 'You're very good at that, aren't you? Fixing things to be how *you* want them.'

'And you, Sunny,' he said in a calm, quiet tone. 'I care very much about how you want them, too.'

'You have no right to decide that for me, Bryce,' she retorted fiercely, inflamed by his air of unshakeable control.

He lifted his hands in appeal. 'What have I decided without discussing it with you?'

'Derek! You stopped him from seeing me and didn't even tell me he'd come to try for a reconciliation.'

His face visibly tightened. The green eyes flared with violent feeling. 'You throw him up at me? A man who knew you so little he could abuse you in terms that I knew were false on just one day's acquaintance with you?'

'How do I know you didn't give him reason to think those things, Bryce? To get rid of him so you'd have a clear running track for what you wanted.'

'Your relationship with him was finished.' He hurled an arm out in savage dismissal. 'You acted on that. Why wouldn't I act on it?'

'He came to see me. Not you. You had no right to...'

'You gave me the right by being in *my* suite, *my* bath...' His eyes glittered with angry possessiveness as they raked her up and down. '...*my* bed!'

Sunny clenched her hands, fighting the sexual power he projected. 'You didn't *own* me, Bryce.'

'You were with me,' he asserted, his eyes burning that undeniable truth straight through her defences. 'Why would I let a drunken fool whom you had rejected, violate the intimacy you were sharing with me?'

Her mind spun on one point she hadn't known. 'He was drunk?'

'And creating trouble.'

'Trouble because you wouldn't let him see me,' she shot at him, determined not to get distracted from the main issue here.

'He had lost the right to demand anything of you, Sunny.'

The mention of *rights* exploded any gain he'd made with his picture of a drunken Derek. She stormed around the suite, putting distance between them, seething at his arrogance in making that judgment. Which he'd clearly made to suit *his purpose*.

Never mind that she'd been hurt by her belief that Derek seemingly hadn't even noticed her absence that night. Bryce hadn't cared about her feelings, except in so far as making them more positive towards him. She swung around to accuse him of it, noting he hadn't moved. He stood tautly watching her, channelling all his energy into working out how to achieve his ends this time.

'The truth is...you weren't going to give him any second chance, were you, Bryce?'

'He'd had his chance with you and blew it,' he grated.

'That was for me to decide.'

She saw him gather himself, shoulders straightening, his formidable chest lifting, strength of mind emanating powerfully from him as he stepped towards her, his gaze holding hers with mesmerising intensity.

'What are you telling me, Sunny? You would have had him back?'

It was a pertinent question, challenging where she stood as he closed on her. Sunny's chin lifted defiantly. Just because she had married him didn't mean she would overlook how he had dealt with possible opposition.

'I'll never know now, will I?' she flung at him. 'I didn't hear what he had to say.'

Bryce kept coming, relentlessly determined on his will prevailing. 'You heard him the next morning,' he pointedly reminded her.

'Yes, I heard him.' Her heart was pounding. He was so big, so indomitable, and one perverse side of her liked the fact he wouldn't be beaten. Yet he shouldn't have taken her choice out of her hands. 'And I wonder now what you said to him the night before.'

'I told him we were negotiating a new position for you in Los Angeles and I didn't care to have our discussion interrupted,' came the imperturbable reply.

'Did he fight that?' she instantly queried, knowing she would have fought, as she was fighting now for integrity in her relationship with Bryce.

'Yes.' Contempt flashed into his eyes. 'He lied, claiming you were his fiancée, which I knew you no longer were. I faced him with the lie and told him you were free to contact him at any time... *if* you wanted to.' His hands curled around her upper arms, pressing his truth. 'But you didn't want to, Sunny. You wanted to be with me.'

'I thought there was nothing left with Derek,' she argued, resenting the way he was boxing her into a corner.

'He's not worth the candle you're burning for him, and you know it,' he insisted. 'You liked what you had with me. You wanted it.'

Her eyes warred with the blazing certainty in his, yet she couldn't deny the wanton desire he stirred in her. 'What I've learnt from this, Bryce, is that you play to win,' she bit out angrily. 'Whatever it takes, you play to win.'

'You're right. I do play to win,' he conceded with ruthless intent. One hand slid up and tangled in her hair at the nape of her neck. 'That's the kind of man you married, Sunny.'

She couldn't bring herself to move or even protest. Her mind screamed it was wrong to feel excited by the electric energy swirling from him, yet her whole body was tingling, and when he spoke again, his voice seemed to throb through her bloodstream.

'I wanted you as my wife. I got you as my wife. And I'll do everything in my power to keep you as my wife.'

Then he kissed her.

CHAPTER FIFTEEN

BRYCE lay awake in the darkness long after Sunny had fallen asleep in his arms. She had responded to him as she always did, caught up in the storm of desire that raged through them, demanding every possible satisfaction. His mind kept hotly buzzing *she was his*. But a more chilling section of his brain acknowledged he had *made* her his.

He had blocked Marsden out and seized the advantage of the rebound effect, refusing to believe that such a stupid loser could possibly be the better man for Sunny. He still didn't believe it. Yet why relationships worked for the people involved was often perplexing to an outside viewpoint. Needs could go right back to a person's roots and seem totally illogical to anyone who hadn't lived that life.

Yes, he'd won the play. Sunny was *his* wife. Yet if her emotions were still tied up with that guy...what did he have? The use of her body. Not long ago he might have thought that was enough. Certainly he'd expected no more from Kristen. But Sunny...

Somehow everything was different with Sunny. He wanted the whole package—heart, body and soul. Why she inspired this craving for all of her he didn't know, but he knew he wouldn't be content until he had it.

The black irony was he'd felt their honeymoon had

moved her much closer to him. It had been a risk coming to Sydney so soon, but it was the appropriate course to take—meeting Sunny's family and collecting what she wanted of her clothes and other possessions—and he'd thought he had the risk covered.

Sherman had straightened Marsden out about the legal consequences of malicious slander and damage during his stopover in Los Angeles. There'd been no loose talk at the Sydney office when he'd resigned—of his own free will, no pressure involved on that front. Bryce hadn't been anticipating any comebacks.

Careful questioning of the managing director had assured him the resignation was interpreted as a matter of pride. And given Marsden's lack of career interest at the conference, he wasn't considered a loss to the company. On the business side, the field had been cleared. It was the personal side that had slipped past him.

Marsden had mouthed off to one of the family.

So who had been tactless enough to face Sunny with her ex-fiancé's rantings? Her mother? No. Too kind-hearted. Alyssa? No. She'd been happily positive about the marriage. He doubted Alyssa would have done anything to take the shine off it. Which left Nadine. Little flashes of envy there. She was the most likely candidate, though she probably hadn't meant to undermine Sunny's confidence in her decision to marry him.

The critical question was how much harm had been done. Certainly Marsden had been brought right back to the forefront of Sunny's mind, and what had been clear-cut on the morning of their wedding day, was now muddied. Somehow he had to get Sunny positive about their marriage again. Wipe Marsden right out of the picture.

She was quiet the next morning. Bryce sensed she was both mentally and emotionally withdrawn from him as she moved about the suite, getting ready for their departure. He controlled his frustration as best he could, but when they sat down to the breakfast delivered by room service, and Sunny persistently evaded his gaze, the urge to confront came thundering into prominence.

'Would you prefer to be married to Marsden?' he growled.

That lifted her eyelashes. It probably wasn't the smartest question to ask but at least it got her attention.

'I'm married to you, Bryce,' she stated flatly, making it an incontravertible fact that was not up for question.

It goaded him into saying, 'Maybe I don't care for the idea of being married to a woman who's hankering after someone else.'

Her eyes flared to an intense gold. 'I'm not *hankering* after Derek. That would be really stupid, wouldn't it? Given the circumstances.'

'I would have thought so, yes,' he answered tersely.

'Do you consider me stupid?'

'No.'

'Then why do you imagine I'm hankering after him?'

'You're angry with me because I didn't allow him a second chance with you. Which suggests you would have liked that.'

She reached for a piece of toast and buttered it with

slow deliberation, her face completely closed to him. 'I might have given Derek a hearing at the time, but that time has gone,' she said, adding strawberry conserve to the toast. 'I chose to marry you and that's where I am…married to you.'

'You were happy about it until yesterday,' he reminded her.

'I didn't understand that it was about winning.' Her gaze flicked up to meet his. 'I'm sorry to report a setback in your winning play this morning.'

He frowned, completely missing what she meant. 'What do you find wrong in my wanting you as my wife?'

Her mouth curled into a wry little smile. 'Possibly the fact that I'm slow off the mark delivering the rest of what you want, Bryce.'

'Which is?' he prompted, still puzzled by her words and needing more insight on where she was coming from.

'I didn't get pregnant on our honeymoon.'

The blunt statement caught him by surprise. His entire thought process had been focused on her feelings for Marsden. He shook his head, his brain whirling to accommodate this new parameter, to fit it into her behaviour and make a different sense of it.

'Believe it, Bryce,' she said dryly, misinterpreting his confusion. 'My period came this morning.'

He watched her bite into the strawberry-laden toast as though she needed a sweetener for the sour taste that piece of news had left in her mouth.

'You're upset because you're not pregnant?' he blurted out, relieved that *this* was the problem.

'It *is* why we got married...to have a child,' she reminded him, her eyes flashing bleak irony.

'That's what you've been holding in from me this morning? You didn't want to tell me?'

'It is...' she grimaced, her eyes dulling further as she added, '...disappointing.'

Bryce instantly reached across the table and took her free hand in his, gently fondling it. 'I'm sorry you're disappointed, Sunny. But it is only early days in our marriage,' he pressed, wanting to console her. 'I'm sure it will happen. It's probably better that you're not pregnant straight off, what with having to settle into a new home and a new job.'

She stared at him in stunned disbelief. 'Aren't *you* disappointed?'

Bryce hadn't stopped to think about it. He paused for a moment, remembering the motivations he'd spelled out to her. Somehow they didn't seem quite so important now. But having a child *was* important to Sunny, he reminded himself before answering.

'We'll make a baby soon enough,' he warmly assured her.

'But...you wanted this for your father,' she said in obvious bewilderment.

'I don't see that you can force nature for anyone,' he answered reasonably.

'You wanted to give him a grandchild before...before...'

'My father is happy that I've married, Sunny. He's seen for himself we're a good match. He knows we intend to have children. It would be good to give him the news that we're expecting a baby, but it doesn't have to be immediate. Another month or two...' He shrugged, wanting to remove her anxiety.

She shook her head, still disturbed. 'I don't understand why I didn't fall pregnant. We...' She flushed, obviously recalling their intense sexual activity.

'Maybe the pills had some lingering influence. Don't worry about it, Sunny.'

'You're not worried by it?' she queried uncertainly.

'No.' He smiled. 'I'm very happy just having you as my wife.'

Sunny searched his eyes, disbelief warring with the sincerity he was projecting. Was this the truth? He wanted her as his wife first, and his father's needs came second?

'Forget about it. Enjoy your breakfast,' he urged, withdrawing his hand to continue his own meal, his whole demeanour beaming good humour. His eyes twinkled wickedly as he added, 'We have a month of high-level energy business ahead of us.'

He *was* happy. There could be no doubting it. The tense silence, which Sunny had to acknowledge causing herself as she'd battled with the emotional conflict of failing to conceive, was completely banished by a stream of plans from Bryce—plans that were clearly coated with pleasurable anticipation.

She was almost giddy with relief. When they finally left for the airport, she didn't mind at all when Bryce took her hand in the now familiar, possessive grip. It felt more like a symbol of togetherness, a warm, secure promise of his commitment to her.

His wife...

Her heart went all mushy at the memory of how

wildly he'd wanted her last night. He'd driven any thought of Derek right out of her mind. Besides, there had been fair reasoning in his argument for having denied Derek a reconciliation bid. Why should he let a potential rival break into the intimacy she had willingly shared with him?

That would have been stupid.

As stupid as her hankering after Derek now.

No way!

She smiled to herself over the realisation that Bryce had been nursing jealous feelings over her supposed lingering attachment to Derek. It wasn't just her body he wanted. Desire was certainly a driving force but there was also a passion for more than sex in their relationship.

A sigh of contentment whispered from her lips, bringing a swift look of concern from Bryce.

'Are you okay, Sunny? If you're in some discomfort from...'

'No.' She smiled to erase any doubt. 'Just glad you're not disappointed.'

He slanted his eyebrows ruefully. 'Well, it does curtail some rather basic pleasures but we'll probably need the rest after this trip anyhow.'

She laughed, happy that he was thinking of just the two of them and not the baby she wasn't having yet.

Next month, she thought.

Next month they would surely have good news to give to his father.

CHAPTER SIXTEEN

FORTUNATELY there was a dispenser carrying sanitary napkins in the ladies' room. Sunny hadn't come to work prepared for such an unwelcome and demoralising eventuality. She had felt absolutely certain she would fall pregnant this month, even buying a pregnancy test kit ready to confirm the fact, counting the days to when it could be used.

Now this...

She hated her body for betraying her. Why couldn't it co-operate with her dearest wish? And how was she going to tell Bryce they had failed again?

A wave of sickening depression rolled through her. It made no sense that she hadn't conceived when they'd been making love every night. Over and over again she had lain in Bryce's arms, smiling, wondering if it was happening...the miracle of life beginning. Happy dreams...

Except they weren't coming true!

Feeling totally wretched, Sunny walked slowly back to the office Bryce had set up for her in the Los Angeles headquarters of Templar Resources. It was a wonderful office. Normally it gave her pleasure to enter this room, knowing Bryce had every confidence in her ability to carry off her new position as head of sales presentations, advising the team under her and monitoring their results. She had enjoyed the challenge of being in charge.

But she wasn't in charge of her body.

The fear of being infertile started hovering. She sat down at her desk and stared blankly at the printout of figures in front of her. Her womb ached with the draining of hope. It was impossible to concentrate on work. All she could think of was not measuring up to motherhood.

If there was something wrong with her...if she couldn't have a baby...what was this marriage worth? She loved Bryce with all her heart, but if she couldn't give him a child...it just wouldn't be right to even try to hang on to him. He wanted children, and not only to satisfy his father.

As it was, time was slipping away on giving his father a grandchild. Would Bryce start thinking Kristen Parrish might have been the better choice of wife? Sunny shuddered at the unbearable thought. He was *her* man, *her* husband. Yet if she couldn't deliver what he wanted...and he had spelled it out before he'd married her...

A hasty marriage.

Repent at leisure.

The words were coming back to haunt her now.

They should have waited. She should have had tests done first. No doubt Bryce would have insisted on tests during his premarital wrangle with his first choice of wife. Sunny couldn't bring herself to question his potency. She was sure it was beyond question. The fault had to lie with her.

Somehow she dragged herself through the rest of

the working day, though she did cancel a meeting she'd scheduled, too aware of not being able to give her best to it. Her head was pounding by the time Bryce came by her office to collect her for the trip home. She looked at him—this man amongst men— and it was totally heart-ravaging to think she couldn't give him the progeny he deserved.

'Something wrong?' he asked, frowning at her, the perceptive green eyes sharply scanning.

She grimaced. 'Raging headache.'

'Have you taken some pain-killers for it?'

'Yes.'

'Let's get you home then. You don't look at all well.' He took her bag from her, ushered her out of the office, then tucked her arm around his, keeping her close to him for support on the walk to the base- ment car park. 'Do you suffer from migraines, Sunny?' he asked gently.

'Not as a rule,' she muttered, feeling horribly guilty for letting his sympathy flow over her instead of tell- ing him the cause of her pain.

'I guess you don't feel like talking,' he said, his understanding making the guilt even worse.

She had to tell him. He had the right to know. It couldn't be hidden anyhow. Sheer misery made her hold her tongue until they were in his car and heading for home, but her sense of fairness forced her to speak at the first long traffic stoppage on the freeway.

'I've got my period again,' she blurted out.

She sensed more than saw his head jerk towards her. Her own gaze was fixed on the road ahead. Her hands were clenched in her lap. She could barely stop herself from bursting into tears.

Then a big warm hand covered hers. 'I'm sorry, Sunny,' came the soft, gruff words. 'I know how much you were counting on being pregnant this time.'

The tears welled and spilled over. She had to bite her lips against breaking into sobs. Speech was impossible. The traffic started moving again and Bryce returned his hand to the driving wheel. She heard him heave a deep sigh and that was the worst thing of all…knowing how he must be feeling now.

Overlooking her first failure was one thing. They'd only been married two weeks and the contraceptive pills she'd been using might have messed up any chance of getting pregnant. There simply wasn't any reason for failing this month. If she was fertile, there should be a baby growing inside her right now. Bryce had to know that as certainly as she did.

She swiped the stream of tears from her cheeks and leaned forward, fumbling in the bag at her feet for some tissues. Her make-up was probably running everywhere. Not only was she a mess inside, she was fast becoming a mess outside, as well. She grabbed the little packet of tissues she always carried with her and sat back again, removing a couple to mop up her face.

'Please don't take it so much to heart, Sunny,' Bryce said quietly. 'It's not unusual for many couples to try for months before…'

'We're not just any couple!' she cried. 'You know we're not.'

He sighed again.

She closed her eyes and willed the tears to dry up.
'I'm sorry,' Bryce murmured. 'If you're worrying
about my father...I just wish you'd stop. I hate seeing
you in this state.'

She took a deep breath, trying to ease the tightness
in her chest. Nothing could ease the pain in her heart.
She understood that Bryce didn't want to see her
weeping. Men were invariably uncomfortable with
displays of deep emotional stress. Apart from which,
he undoubtedly had his own inner dismay to deal
with. He'd married her to have a child, the child was
not forthcoming, and it was certainly not from any
slack performance on his part.

Sunny had no idea how long it took to drive to
their home in Santa Monica. Bryce remained silent
and her mind was in a total ferment. Only the rolling
open of the garage door, triggered by the remote de-
vice in the car, alerted her to the fact that the journey
was over and facing up to the situation with Bryce
was now imminent.

Her legs were hopelessly shaky as she walked
ahead of him along the short hallway that led from
the garage to the space-age kitchen with its gleaming
stainless steel surfaces. Her churning stomach refuted
any idea of food. Preparing any dinner for them was
beyond her tonight. She went past the kitchen, wishing she could make a bolt for the staircase and a bed
where she could curl up and quietly die, but there
really was no hiding place.

'Sunny...'

The concern and soft appeal in Bryce's voice
forced her to stop halfway across the open-plan living

area. She took a deep breath, straightened her spine, and swung to look back at him. He'd halted by the kitchen serving bench. He gestured towards the refrigerator.

'Can I get you anything?'

Her heart turned over. He wanted to do something for her...help...but there was no help for this.

'A cup of tea?' he suggested, knowing she preferred it to coffee.

'Do you know where I should go to have a fertility test, Bryce?' she asked, determined on not evading the issue.

'Yes, but...' He looked pained by the question.

'I'll go next week. If it turns out that I'm...I'm barren...' What a terrible word that was, so redolent of empty devastation!

'You don't need to put yourself through this, Sunny,' he protested.

'Yes, I do. Both of us need to know if I can or can't have a baby.'

He shook his head.

'If I can't, Bryce, we get a divorce as soon as possible.'

'No!' The negative was harsh and explosive.

Sunny ignored it. 'I won't take you for anything. What's yours will remain yours. You can trust me on that. I'll just go back to Australia and get on with my life.'

'Money has nothing to do with it!' he fiercely claimed.

'I'm glad you understand that,' Sunny shot back at him, undeterred by his vehemence. 'It never did for me,' she continued flatly. 'But a child matters, Bryce. If I can't give you one, it's best we part now.'

'No!' he repeated strongly.

She looked at him with deadly calm washed out eyes. 'You know it. I know it. That's how it is.'

He stared back, his black brows beetled down over eyes burning with the need to wipe out all she'd said. But he couldn't. The equation was irrefutable.

Sunny turned away, forcing her tremulous legs to take one step after another, increasing the distance between them as she made her way up the stairs to the bedroom where their mating had been a delusion. It had not borne fruit. An empty bed...but a soft pillow to bury her misery in.

Bryce watched her walk away from him, too stunned by the bald words she had spoken to make any move. All he could think of was...*did he mean so little to her?*

He didn't want a divorce. Not for any reason. They'd been married almost two months and it had been the best two months of his entire life. He'd felt...truly not alone anymore. Not that he had ever really dwelled on loneliness. He'd considered himself self-sufficient.

But Sunny had filled all the empty spaces that he hadn't even recognised before she came into his life...filled them with warmth and joy, giving him a sheer pleasure in being, in having her with him, in sharing all the things he'd never really shared with anyone.

Divorce!

For the sake of some theoretical child he might have with a Kristen-like replacement?

Could such a child make up for a *barren* marriage?

Everything within Bryce shouted *no!*

He'd just paid out a fortune to be rid of Kristen Parrish and her self-righteous claims, a costly mistake for choosing her in the first place. But choosing Sunny was no mistake. Child or no child, he couldn't bear to even think of living the rest of his life without her.

She was his wife.

His wife in every sense.

He'd won her and nothing was going to stop him from keeping her.

Nothing!

His feet started moving. The adrenaline rush of going into battle carried him up the stairs at a pace that brooked no opposition. He was going to smash any barriers Sunny put up. He would hold her to him, no matter what! His whole body bristled with the ferocity of his feeling. He strode into their bedroom, intent on fighting with everything he could fight with, his heart thundering with the need to win.

One look at Sunny and his intent was instantly blown to pieces. She was scrunched up on the bed, her back turned to him, a back that was heaving with sobs, muffled by the pillow her face was pushed into. She was hugging another pillow for comfort. She'd kicked off her shoes and there was something terribly vulnerable about her stockinged feet, tucked up and rubbing against each other as though they were cold.

It struck him forcefully that this was grief. Heart-breaking grief. Was it possible that she didn't want their marriage to end any more than he did? Maybe she just couldn't see over the hump of not having a child. He couldn't say it didn't matter because it did to her. She wanted to be a mother. But if she couldn't be, he was still her husband and she was still his wife and he had to show her that what they had together was still worth having.

Quietly he took off his suitcoat and tie and dropped them on a chair, freeing himself of constriction. He moved over to the bed, resting one knee on the side of it to get his balance right, then slid his arms under Sunny, scooping her up against his chest, then swinging around to sit and cradle her on his lap.

'Bryce...' she choked out shakily.

'Hush now,' he soothed, pressing her head onto his shoulder and stroking her hair, trying to impart warmth and comfort. 'I want to hold you. I need to hold you, Sunny.'

She shuddered and sagged limply into the cocoon of his embrace, her strength all spent in trying to play straight with him. He simply held her for a while, stroking away the little tremors that shook her, thinking of all she meant to him.

He loved the rare integrity of her heart and mind— her whole character—the way she threw all of herself into whatever she took on, her openness and her honesty. He loved her innate decency, her caring, her sharing. He loved the feel of her, the scent of her, the wonderful sexuality of her. She was his wife.

'I want you to listen to me, Sunny,' he appealed softly. 'Just hear me out...'

*   *   *

She simply didn't have the energy to argue anymore. It was easier to let his words float over her because they couldn't really mean anything. It felt bittersweet being held like this, kindly, protectively, but for a little while she wanted to wallow in the sense of closeness, of Bryce caring for her.

'I know you want to be a mother,' he started slowly. 'I think you should go and have a fertility test next week so you'll know beyond any doubt if motherhood is on the cards for you. This fear you have…you're letting it eat you up, Sunny, letting it take over as though you're not worth anything if you can't have a baby. And that's not true.'

He wasn't getting it right, she thought wearily. It wasn't the end of the world for her if she had to be childless, but it would be the end of her world with him. Why was he holding off from seeing that?

'You're worth a great deal to me,' he continued gruffly. 'You've given me more than I ever imagined any one person could give another. You've shown me…what a woman in a man's life can mean to him…in so many ways…and on so many levels…'

His voice seemed to throb into her mind, his words like slow, deep heartbeats, pulsing with the very essence of *his* life. She was stirred out of the apathy she had fallen into. Her ears prickled with the need to listen, to hear every shade of what he was saying.

His chest rose and fell as he gathered more of his thoughts. 'My father…'

A sick tension gripped Sunny again at the mention of Will Templar.

'My father…is my father.'

He spoke as if searching for a truth he needed to communicate. She found herself holding her breath, listening with every atom of energy she had.

'He's been the only real constant in my life…all my life. And I do feel…an undeniable bond with him. He's my father…'

And they were very alike, very much father and son…a bond that would never be broken, she thought, and one she couldn't fight.

'But you're my wife, Sunny…and I love you. I love you as I've never loved any other person.'

He *loved* her?

'I didn't know what love was…how it could be…'

He swept his mouth over her hair, pressing warm, lingering kisses as though wanting, needing to imprint his feeling on her, and Sunny started tingling with the sweet joy of it, unable to cling to any fearful caution.

'But I do now with you,' he went on fervently. 'And I don't want to lose it. Ever…'

She didn't, either.

'If we can't have a child…believe me, Sunny…I don't want a child with any other woman. You are more important to me than any child could ever be. Having *you* sharing my life…that comes first. I promise you…it will always come first.'

She was swamped by his caring…caring for her…only her…

His hand threaded through her hair and cradled her head, his fingers gently kneading as he made his last bid for the marriage he wanted.

'You said love to you was emotional security. I

don't know what more to do…to prove you have that with me, Sunny.' He took a deep breath and poured out his heart. 'Please…I love you so much. Can you let this pregnancy issue go, and just…*be* with me?'

How could she not?

She loved him.

CHAPTER SEVENTEEN

SUNNY gazed in adoring fascination at the baby snuggled in the crook of her arm. Her baby. Hers and Bryce's. He was so beautiful, she couldn't stop smiling.

It was possible to look back now and be glad she hadn't fallen pregnant in those first couple of months of their marriage. To Sunny's mind, it was so much better having their child a true child of love and not the result of a marriage bargain. And that was how it had happened in the end.

The most probable cause of her initial infertility was anxiety, the doctor had told her—wanting to get it right for Bryce and his father. There'd been nothing physically wrong with her. Once she had felt emotionally secure in her marriage, she had fallen pregnant the very next month. And here she was...a mother at last.

The footsteps coming along the hospital corridor heralded Bryce's return from the airport. A glance at her watch assured her the time was about right. The clacking heels undoubtedly belonged to her mother who had flown from Sydney to see her new grandchild and stay for a while to give Sunny any help she might need in getting used to motherhood. Voices became more decipherable and she heard Will Templar giving forth.

'Oh, I knew it would be a boy. No surprise at all.'

Sunny rolled her eyes at her father-in-law's smug confidence. His flight from Sedona must have come in at approximately the same time as her mother's for them to have all met up together.

'Bryce was bound to have sons,' he went on proudly.

Sunny almost wished she'd had a daughter. Will Templar was far too fond of getting his own way. Not that she'd swap her darling little boy for any other baby. He had his tiny hand curled around her little finger, and while he might be too young to focus properly, he seemed to be looking straight into her eyes, loving her right back.

Bryce popped his head around the door and grinned at her. 'Ready for visitors?'

'It's showtime,' she said, grinning back at him.

In came her mother, beaming excitement and carrying a big bunch of irises and daffodils. 'Sunny... you look wonderful! And here he is...' She set the flowers on the bed, gave Sunny a kiss, and swept the baby up to cradle him herself. 'Oh, what a bonny boy!'

'Looks just like Bryce,' Will declared, peering over her shoulder.

'Nonsense!' her mother chided indulgently. 'See those curls? He's got Sunny's hair.'

'But it's black, like Bryce's,' Will pointed out, sticking to his judgment.

'Will, your son does not have curls,' her mother said firmly.

'Chip off the old block anyway,' Will muttered.

'Lucky your daughter's got brains as well as beauty, Marion. What we have here is a fine set of genes.'

'There's no luck involved at all, Will. Sunny married a man who matched her.'

'Well, can't go wrong with that combination,' he conceded. 'They're a good pairing. Saw it straight away.'

'Yes. They struck me that way, too. Very much in love.'

It was clear Will Templar considered this a soppy sentiment. 'What's love got to do with it?'

Her mother gave him an archly knowing look. 'Everything.' Then she smiled her perfect understanding at her daughter. 'What are you calling him, Sunny?'

'Adam,' she answered, giving Bryce a quizzical glance that encompassed their separate parents.

He rolled his eyes back at her, indicating there'd been a running altercation between them all the way here.

'Good strong name,' Will approved.

'Yes. It goes well with Templar,' her mother agreed.

'He's my grandson, too, you know,' Will reminded her mother. 'How about letting me hold him?'

'I think you'd better sit down first,' Marion York advised him. 'Sunny told me you had a heart condition.'

'Doctors are fixing that up. Gave me a whole heap of new drugs and they're working,' he declared. 'Do I look like a man with a heart condition?'

In truth, Bryce's father was looking surprisingly well, Sunny thought. He'd put on some weight and his face was a much better colour.

'Well, I must say you look like a man in his prime, Will,' Marion said admiringly, and Will Templar instantly puffed out his chest. She smiled winningly as she added, 'But why not sit down anyway? Much easier to handle a baby sitting down. You haven't had as much practice at it as I have.'

'True. But I'll have you know this grandchild is giving me a new lease on life.' He settled himself in one of the armchairs. 'Give him here.'

Sunny and Bryce exchanged highly amused looks as her mother carefully handed their baby son over to his grandfather who immediately started rocking him to show he knew exactly what a baby liked.

'Isn't he lovely?' her mother cooed.

'A real boy,' Will declared.

Her mother straightened up, positively glowing. She was wearing a plum-coloured pantsuit, a skivvy in a soft shade of wheat, a pretty scarf with a swirl of purple and plum and gold. The colours looked wonderful on her, and her eyes were sparkling, no sign at all that she'd just endured a long flight from Sydney.

'I'll go and find a vase for these flowers, Sunny. Though I don't know where we're going to put them,' she added ruefully, gazing around at the flower-filled room. 'Did Bryce buy out all the florist shops in Los Angeles?'

'Only the red roses are from me,' Bryce told her. 'Sunny has a knack of making lots of friends.'

'We can move something, Mum,' Sunny assured her. 'I love the irises and daffodils.'

'Good!' She gathered up the bouquet. 'I won't be long, dear.'

Off she went with Will Templar gazing after her admiringly before commenting to Sunny, 'Fine-looking woman, your mother. Think I'll stay on in L.A. and make sure she enjoys herself here.'

'Dad, you do have to take care with that heart of yours,' Bryce quietly reminded him.

It earned a flash of proud defiance. 'I'm not dead yet, boy.' He looked down at his new grandson. 'He's the future but I'm still very much alive,' he muttered. 'No reason I can't take a sixth wife.'

Bryce and Sunny burst into laughter.

The new grandfather didn't understand their amusement.

'You wouldn't want to be doing anything hasty, Dad,' Bryce advised with mock solemnity.

'No,' said Sunny. 'A hasty marriage might not work.'

'Did for you,' Will Templar argued. 'I don't see you two repenting at leisure.'

'No repentance at all,' Bryce agreed.

'And not likely to be,' Sunny chimed in.

Whereupon, Bryce sat on the bed next to her and drew her into his embrace. 'Hi, new Mom,' he murmured.

'Hi, new Dad,' she answered, winding her arms around his neck. 'I love you Bryce Templar, and I still fancy you rotten.'

'Likewise.'

Then he kissed her.

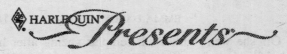

by Catherine George

A family with a passion for life— and for love.

Get to know the Dysarts!
Over the coming months you can share
the dramas and joys, and hopes and dreams
of this wealthy English family, as unexpected
passions, births and marriages unfold
in their lives.

LORENZO'S REWARD
Harlequin Presents® #2203
on sale September 2001

RESTLESS NIGHTS
Harlequin Presents® #2244
on sale April 2002

Available wherever Harlequin books are sold.

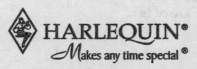

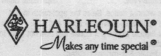

*Harlequin truly does
make any time special. . . .
This year we are celebrating
weddings in style!*

A Walk Down the Aisle
WEDDING CELEBRATION

To help us celebrate, we want you to tell us how wearing the Harlequin wedding gown will make your wedding day special. As the grand prize, Harlequin will offer one lucky bride the chance to **"Walk Down the Aisle"** in the Harlequin wedding gown!

There's more...

For her honeymoon, she and her groom will spend five nights at the **Hyatt Regency Maui.** As part of this five-night honeymoon at the hotel renowned for its romantic attractions, the couple will enjoy a candlelit dinner for two in Swan Court, a sunset sail on the hotel's catamaran, and duet spa treatments.

A HYATT RESORT AND SPA   Maui • Molokai • Lanai

To enter, please write, in, 250 words or less, how wearing the Harlequin wedding gown will make your wedding day special. The entry will be judged based on its emotionally compelling nature, its originality and creativity, and its sincerity. This contest is open to Canadian and U.S. residents only and to those who are 18 years of age and older. There is no purchase necessary to enter. Void where prohibited. See further contest rules attached. Please send your entry to:

Walk Down the Aisle Contest

In Canada	In U.S.A.
P.O. Box 637	P.O. Box 9076
Fort Erie, Ontario	3010 Walden Ave.
L2A 5X3	Buffalo, NY 14269-9076

You can also enter by visiting www.eHarlequin.com
Win the Harlequin wedding gown and the vacation of a lifetime!
The deadline for entries is October 1, 2001.

HARLEQUIN®
Makes any time special ®

PHWDACONT1

HARLEQUIN WALK DOWN THE AISLE TO MAUI CONTEST 1197
OFFICIAL RULES
NO PURCHASE NECESSARY TO ENTER

1. To enter, follow directions published in the offer to which you are responding. Contest begins April 2, 2001, and ends on October 1, 2001. Method of entry may vary. Mailed entries must be postmarked by October 1, 2001, and received by October 8, 2001.

2. Contest entry may be, at times, presented via the Internet, but will be restricted solely to residents of certain geographic areas that are disclosed on the Web site. To enter via the Internet, if permissible, access the Harlequin Web site (www.eHarlequin.com) and follow the directions displayed online. Online entries must be received by 11:59 p.m. E.S.T. on October 1, 2001.

   In lieu of submitting an entry online, enter by mail by hand-printing (or typing) on an 8½" x 11" plain piece of paper, your name, address (including zip code), Contest number/name and in 250 words or fewer, why winning a Harlequin wedding dress would make your wedding day special. Mail via first-class mail to: Harlequin Walk Down the Aisle Contest 1197, (in the U.S.) P.O. Box 9076, 3010 Walden Avenue, Buffalo, NY 14269-9076, (in Canada) P.O. Box 637, Fort Erie, Ontario L2A 5X3, Canada.

   Limit one entry per person, household address and e-mail address. Online and/or mailed entries received from persons residing in geographic areas in which Internet entry is not permissible will be disqualified.

3. Contests will be judged by a panel of members of the Harlequin editorial, marketing and public relations staff based on the following criteria:

   - Originality and Creativity—50%
   - Emotionally Compelling—25%
   - Sincerity—25%

   In the event of a tie, duplicate prizes will be awarded. Decisions of the judges are final.

4. All entries become the property of Torstar Corp. and will not be returned. No responsibility is assumed for lost, late, illegible, incomplete, inaccurate, nondelivered or misdirected mail or misdirected e-mail, for technical, hardware or software failures of any kind, lost or unavailable network connections, or failed, incomplete, garbled or delayed computer transmission or any human error which may occur in the receipt or processing of the entries in this Contest.

5. Contest open only to residents of the U.S. (except Puerto Rico) and Canada, who are 18 years of age or older, and is void wherever prohibited by law; all applicable laws and regulations apply. Any litigation within the Province of Quebec respecting the conduct or organization of a publicity contest may be submitted to the Régie des alcools, des courses et des jeux for a ruling. Any litigation respecting the awarding of a prize may be submitted to the Régie des alcools, des courses et des jeux only for the purpose of helping the parties reach a settlement. Employees and immediate family members of Torstar Corp. and D. L. Blair, Inc., their affiliates, subsidiaries and all other agencies, entities and persons connected with the use, marketing or conduct of this Contest are not eligible to enter. Taxes on prizes are the sole responsibility of winners. Acceptance of any prize offered constitutes permission to use winner's name, photograph or other likeness for the purposes of advertising, trade and promotion on behalf of Torstar Corp., its affiliates and subsidiaries without further compensation to the winner, unless prohibited by law.

6. Winners will be determined no later than November 15, 2001, and will be notified by mail. Winners will be required to sign and return an Affidavit of Eligibility form within 15 days after winner notification. Noncompliance within that time period may result in disqualification and an alternative winner may be selected. Winners of trip must execute a Release of Liability prior to ticketing and must possess required travel documents (e.g. passport, photo ID) where applicable. Trip must be completed by November 2002. No substitution of prize permitted by winner. Torstar Corp. and D. L. Blair, Inc., their parents, affiliates, and subsidiaries are not responsible for errors in printing or electronic presentation of Contest, entries and/or game pieces. In the event of printing or other errors which may result in unintended prize values or duplication of prizes, all affected game pieces or entries shall be null and void. If for any reason the Internet portion of the Contest is not capable of running as planned, including infection by computer virus, bugs, tampering, unauthorized intervention, fraud, technical failures, or any other causes beyond the control of Torstar Corp. which corrupt or affect the administration, secrecy, fairness, integrity or proper conduct of the Contest, Torstar Corp. reserves the right, at its sole discretion, to disqualify any individual who tampers with the entry process and to cancel, terminate, modify or suspend the Contest or the Internet portion thereof. In the event of a dispute regarding an online entry, the entry will be deemed submitted by the authorized holder of the e-mail account submitted at the time of entry. Authorized account holder is defined as the natural person who is assigned to an e-mail address by an Internet access provider, online service provider or other organization that is responsible for arranging e-mail address for the domain associated with the submitted e-mail address. **Purchase or acceptance of a product offer does not improve your chances of winning.**

7. Prizes: (1) Grand Prize—A Harlequin wedding dress (approximate retail value: $3,500) and a 5-night/6-day honeymoon trip to Maui, HI, including round-trip air transportation provided by Maui Visitors Bureau from Los Angeles International Airport (winner is responsible for transportation to and from Los Angeles International Airport) and a Harlequin Romance Package, including hotel accomodations (double occupancy) at the Hyatt Regency Maui Resort and Spa, dinner for (2) two at Swan Court, a sunset sail on Kiele V and a spa treatment for the winner (approximate retail value: $4,000); (5) Five runner-up prizes of a $1000 gift certificate to selected retail outlets to be determined by Sponsor (retail value $1000 ea.). Prizes consist of only those items listed as part of the prize. Limit one prize per person. All prizes are valued in U.S. currency.

8. For a list of winners (available after December 17, 2001) send a self-addressed, stamped envelope to: Harlequin Walk Down the Aisle Contest 1197 Winners, P.O. Box 4200 Blair, NE 68009-4200 or you may access the www.eHarlequin.com Web site through January 15, 2002.

Contest sponsored by Torstar Corp., P.O. Box 9042, Buffalo, NY 14269-9042, U.S.A.

PHWDACONT2

Coming Next Month

THE BEST HAS JUST GOTTEN BETTER!

#2199 DUARTE'S CHILD Lynne Graham
Only days before she gave birth, Emily left her husband,
Duarte de Monteiro. Now Duarte has traced her and his baby
son, and brought them back to Portugal—because he loves her,
or just because he wants his son?

#2200 TO MAKE A MARRIAGE Carole Mortimer
Andie is convinced her baby's father is in love with another
woman. But Adam Monroe is also a close family friend—Andie
knows she can't avoid him forever....

#2201 MISTRESS BY CONTRACT Helen Bianchin
There was only one way for Mikayla to clear her father's debt to
tycoon Rafael Velez-Aguilera: offer herself in exchange! Rafael
was intrigued by Mikayla's proposal, and immediately specified
her duties as his mistress for a year!

#2202 THE ALVARES BRIDE Sandra Marton
No one knew the father of Carin's baby—but during the birth
she called out a name: Raphael Alvares! The powerful Brazilian
millionaire rushed to Carin's bedside—but had he come because
the one passionate night they'd shared had left him longing to
make Carin his bride?

#2203 LORENZO'S REWARD Catherine George
When Lorenzo Forli proposed, Jess had no qualms about letting
her husband-to-be make passionate love to her. But Lorenzo had
failed to tell Jess something about his past. Could it be that he'd
used all the means he possessed only to seduce her into his bed?

#2204 TERMS OF ENGAGEMENT Kathryn Ross
In order to avoid her ex-husband, Emma had introduced
Frazer McClarren as her new fiancé. Time and time again they
were forced to play the happy couple, but Emma could not
truly get involved with Frazer—she could never give him what
he wanted....